YULETIDE SLAY RIDE

BRIAN AND MINA'S HOLIDAY HITS
BOOK FOUR

KITTY THOMAS

YULETIDE SLAY RIDE

KITTY THOMAS

Burlesque Press

Thank you to another Brian whose example helped me come back to myself, break out of my block, and inspired me to remain true to my art.

1

BRIAN

Gregor tries to reason with me, but it's far too late for that. The only sound I hear is the musical notes of the chainsaw firing up, the soothing sound of this most perfect machine ripping through his arm, his horrified scream as though he didn't really believe it would happen. No one ever really believes their own death—even if they're watching and feeling it happen right in that moment.

It makes sense. You've never died before, so even though other people die around you, you think it will never be your turn. Or you'll die peacefully in your sleep and never even know about it a long long time from now—when you're eighty-three. Gregor goes into shock before he acknowledges that this is really happening. I hate that he's able to leave this world in such denial. And then, another slice or two later he's dead.

How anticlimactic.

I thought this would be more satisfying, but it was far too quick. I should have picked another method, savored his death, dragged it out. Fuck professional courtesy, he touched Mina. He *kissed* Mina. He put his filthy mouth on her flesh. And she *let* him.

I'm hypnotized by the sound of the saw as it slices through him over and over, as though it's possessed, as though I'm not the one wielding it. I feel like I'm watching all this happen from the outside instead of doing it myself. It's as if my weapon of choice is a self-aware living thing, and I'm only witnessing the carnage.

He's all just so much meat now, but still, I keep hacking away. At least I can horrify his soul as it watches from above. There has to be some basic level of distress watching your own body being hacked up, even if you're on the other side. I don't know if I believe in an afterlife, but if I can trap his soul here in the horror of his own macabre death, I'll take it.

As I continue it becomes a game of "How much blood can I get all over Windsor's nice conservatory?" I suddenly wish I'd had the self control to wait, to let Windsor watch this, and then take him out, slowly, methodically... with surgical precision. It's been a long time since I've used the surgical instruments on a kill.

"That's enough!"

Mina's voice pulls my attention away from the under-whelming experience of spraying Gregor's guts all over the conservatory walls. I turn slowly toward her, and that thin frail hope that I'd held onto... the hope that I could sate the demon raging within me and cool off my simmering rage by hacking up Gregor... that I could spare Mina my evil tonight... that hope is gone.

She feels the shift in me. She knows she isn't safe. She turns... and runs. I almost cackle with glee. It's been so long since I've been able to chase down prey like this. I rev the chainsaw a few times. It has the intended effect, causing her to run even faster, and then without my conscious choice, my feet are moving and I'm chasing her through the cool, crisp night.

What will I do when I catch this little rabbit?

Gregor touched her. He kissed her.

And she let him.

Gregor *touched* her. He *kissed* her.

And she *let* him.

These thoughts repeat over and over in my mind in an obsessive rhythm in time with my feet pounding on the ground. Is she even truly mine anymore? My mind is full of the red haze of blood and death, and the thought that if I can't truly have her, I can *end* her. That's something only between the two of us that no one else can ever have or touch or share. There is nothing more intimate than being the person who removes someone else from this world. And some completely inhuman piece of me craves this dark intimacy.

I try to shove these crazy thoughts out of my head, but they continue to play, taunting me, tempting me to give into my darkness. I'm not a relationship guy. I can't give her what she needs. So why not? Why not do the monstrous thing everyone has always expected of me anyway? It's why Lindsay tried to keep her from me. I'm too damaged to be loved. I'm too damaged to have something as bright and lovely as Mina.

She will never be as bad as me, and we both know it. I can only ever pollute the light left inside her.

Maybe she and Gregor can just go live happily ever after together in the afterlife, frolicking through some field of lilacs somewhere. The full moon illuminates my path as I run through the pumpkin patch. When I'm almost on her, I turn off the chainsaw and fling it away from me.

Whatever I do... it needs to be more intimate than a chainsaw, more personal... maybe my hands around her delicate throat. I tackle her to the ground in the thick soft fat leaves between the pumpkins, and flip her onto her back.

She's terrified. Even her first night at the house when she wandered down to my lair... when I sniffed her and told her to run, she wasn't this scared. Even the day I bought her, when we reached my dungeon room and the blindfold came off, and she realized the monster she now belonged to... she wasn't this scared. But she didn't know the half of what I was back then.

She does now.

I wrap my gloved hand around her throat, feeling her pulse beating hard against my fingertips. I pull it back to find a bloody handprint.

Fucking Gregor, touching her again, marking her with his blood. I tilt my head to the side and just stare down at her, taking slow deep breaths, trying to steady my increasingly erratic thoughts.

"Brian?"

Oh she's really scared now. There are a million things I want to say to her, but my brain refuses to come up with a coherent sentence or quippy retort. All the banter has died. Instead I just flip her over onto her hands and knees and pull her pants and panties down. I smack her ass hard. She should not be wearing panties. We talked about this.

Before I can stop myself, I'm inside her, and her warm liquid heat steals the remaining sanity from my mind.

I gasp, pulling in the breath my dream stole from me as I sit upright in bed. My heart hammers in my throat. Mina stirs beside me.

"Brian?"

Her voice calls out to me in the darkness, but it's not the terror she displayed on Halloween night, it's concern. It's *care* for me. I can't fucking stand it. I lost control and almost killed her. She doesn't know that, though. It was easy enough to focus on the crime of fucking her through her tears. No, I can't trust myself to fuck her. But that one rabid decision may be the only reason she's still breathing.

She's just not safe with me. How can I keep her safe when I'm the biggest threat?

I turn on the lamp and get up and go to the dresser. I pull out a pair of sweat pants and a T-shirt, socks, and running shoes.

Mina starts to get up, too.

"No. Stay. I need to be alone."

I turn to see the tears shining behind her eyes, but I ignore it. Yes, I'm pulling away... somebody has to. How can she sleep beside such a monster every night? How can she snuggle up beside me in the dark? How can she trust me when I don't trust myself?

When I reach the gym, I turn on the Chopin and start running on one of the treadmills. This music doesn't go with blood and screams, but it's what I see and hear as I run. The two incongruent sounds blend and twirl together until it almost makes sense—until they almost belong together. My yin and my yang dancing together on the air just outside my reach.

My running shoes hit the treadmill harder, and louder, faster... but I can't shut it off. The sounds, the blood, Mina. Chasing her through that pumpkin patch while everything inside me called for her blood. I'm too broken. I should be put down.

I shouldn't even be allowed to exist in this world.

I run until I'm exhausted. I just want to stop the sounds and images, all the thoughts that ran through my mind, thoughts I barely remember thinking... of all the ways I wanted to remove her from this world. But it wasn't me... I don't want her gone. I'm not some crazed jealous abusive boyfriend. I wasn't mad at her. I know she did nothing wrong.

It was the wild in me. The dark in me. It was the other, the something else that isn't me, the broken shards of what I became so long ago.

The animal. The monster. That inhuman thing.

There is no saving me.

2

MINA

I turn the lamp back off and lie in the quiet stillness of the dungeon room. It's been three weeks since Halloween night and piece by piece, every day Brian slips away from me a little more. He won't meet my gaze, won't touch me, barely speaks to me.

He hasn't told me what the nightmares are about, but I know. He can't forgive himself for Halloween. I'm surprised he hasn't run off on a personal job and left me behind—or gone hunting to *create* a personal job. Brian doesn't require a contract or a directive to kill.

I lie in the dark forever, waiting for him to come back, wondering if he'll get back in bed and fall asleep beside me, giving me the one unguarded moment when I can press my body against his and pretend things are the same, that we're fine. How did we get here?

And how do we get back?

I finally drift off again into dreamless sleep and when I wake, I turn to find the glaring red numbers on the digital clock say eleven am. I turn on the lamp. Brian's side of the bed is exactly as he left it when he got up to go run. He's not coming back. I try not to let it bother me. He'll get over this; he has to. But I cry in the shower anyway.

Once I've had enough of feeling sorry for myself, I put on some leggings, furry boots, and a sweater. I put a 9mm and several extra magazines in holsters on my waistband and make my way upstairs to join the rest of the house.

I grab some food from the kitchen and wander the grounds. The girls and the trainers stare at me as I pass, including the new girl, Julie. Gabe's girl. Though is she really Gabe's? It doesn't seem like it to me.

They all know something's wrong, but no one dares ask. They've still got enough healthy fear of the new me to prevent that.

I find Brian out in the woods where I knew he'd be, throwing rounds down his homemade gun range. Glass shatters in perfect time as he goes down the row, taking out six bottles, changing magazines, and then taking out the remaining six.

"For fuck's sake," I say when he removes his hearing protection. "I need you to get over this."

He rounds on me, eyes blazing with far more fury than I expected, but I'm so tired of this mope-y Brian. Since when does he have guilt about anything? And I know that's what it is. He can't forgive himself for something that didn't happen.

I never told him no. I never wanted him to stop. It's unnatural for him to be this worked up about this.

"You wouldn't say that if you knew," he says, cryptically.

"Knew what!? Jesus, Brian, whatever it is, just say it. Say it so we can get past it!"

"There's no getting past it."

"That's not for you to decide!"

His gaze narrows on me, and I can see when the decision is made. "Fine. But you asked for this. Just remember you could have remained blissfully ignorant."

Oh, yes, it's been total bliss.

Another full minute passes before he sighs and says, "I almost killed you. I wanted to."

I just blink at him.

"Because I let Gregor kiss me?"

Brian scrubs a hand through his hair. "No. I just... I can't explain it. It's not rational."

"But you didn't. You didn't even hurt me. We all have dark thoughts, Brian. But you didn't act on them. That's what's important."

"You have no idea how close I came."

That admission sends a chill through me, but I know what he's doing. He's trying to scare me. He's punishing himself for something he didn't do because I refused to. So in a way, maybe he's punishing me. But I don't think he'd see it that way.

He brushes past me. "I'm going back to the house. Don't follow me."

I stare after him and resist the urge to crumple to the ground and cry some more. Of all the feelings Brian has brought out in me since I returned from Japan, the one that slices the deepest is this grief at the way he's pulled away.

It wasn't immediate. That first night when we got back from the Windsor estate, I thought we were okay—or that we would be. And nothing was noticeable for the first few days because we were busy planning and taking care of Gabe's job.

The big take down of Dmitri's house. It was personal to Gabe but he paid us handsomely for the work. He'd been hung up on Julie several months before but lost track of her. He'd stopped pursuing her and let her go because she was too sweet and innocent for his darker brand of sex and desire, a fact I don't disagree with judging from their current state of limbo.

When he found her again, she'd been kidnapped and was being trafficked in Dmitri's house—prostituted out to all his gross associates. Dmitri had made our house an offer of partnership and Gabe was sent to go check it out, not knowing the full details of the way they were running their business. When he got there and found Julie, he'd requested she be brought to him for the night but ended up buying her to get her out of there.

Three days after Halloween, Brian and I took down their house and killed Dmitri and all his associates. I made an anonymous call to the police to get the girls to safety that night.

But Julie and Gabe still aren't really together. And right now it feels like Brian and I aren't really together. Anton and Annette seem to be the only happy couple at the moment.

Somehow despite my best intentions, a few stray tears have made their way down my cheeks. I swipe them away with the back of my hand then glance to the side and notice several bottles gathered beside one of the trees. Brian and I collect them from the cafeteria at the end of each day.

Phyllis wanted to send them to recycling, but we decided we'd recycle them into target practice. I'm sure he was planning to go through all of them before I showed up to bust up his guilt party. I pick up a handheld broom and brush stray shards of glass off the tree stumps, then I carefully line my bottles up.

I shoot until I run out of ammo, but my aim is not nearly as good as Brian's when I'm upset. I shoot more trees than bottles —sending birds scattering and squawking as they abandon their trees—though I do get the satisfaction of at least breaking a few.

"Fuck this," I say to the now empty forest. I'm not letting Brian ignore me. He wants to be punished? He wants to pay for the crime of having a bad thought? Fine.

Wish fucking granted.

I holster the 9mm and go back to the house, ignoring the startled looks on everybody's faces as I blaze past them with new purpose. Brian told me not to follow him, but fuck him. He can't ban me from my own room. He's getting over this shit one way or another.

He's in the shower when I reach our dungeon room. Good. I input the code for the weapons room and return my gun to the drawer I took it from. I'll have to remember to clean it later. Brian is religious about cleaning his guns after each use, and it's probably why he's just now gotten into the shower. But right now, I have other priorities.

I press my palm against one of the stones in the wall, and a thinner hidden drawer slides out with all of Brian's syringes— several already prepped and ready to go.

He's just getting out of the shower, toweling off, and wiping the steam from the bathroom mirror when he spots me.

"Mina, I thought I told you not to..."

But he doesn't get the rest out. He catches the shiny glint of the needle in the mirror just before I jab it in his neck. He goes down like an elephant.

And then I'm left with the realization that he may as well *be* an elephant, because there's no way I'm going to be able to get him out of here. I was fueled a little too much on fury and not enough on logistics.

I try to drag him, but he is really big. You don't stop to consider just how heavy such a tall and well-muscled man is, and his height makes him even more impossible to move. I pause, my gaze lingering over his ass. I'm so tempted to touch him, but that feels a little rape-y to me, so I resist the urge. He's completely vulnerable and helpless right now, and I feel a responsibility to respect that.

But he won't be for long. I've got probably forty-five minutes before he snaps out of it and there is hell to pay. The drugs are supposed to last an hour, but I'm pretty sure he'll shake it off sooner, and then I'm in big trouble.

I panic as it fully sinks in that I really can't move him, and the clock is ticking. Like I cannot budge him at all. I use all my strength to move him an inch. At this rate he'll definitely come to well before I can get him anywhere to start enacting the rest of my barely cobbled together plan.

Fuck me. *Okay, think Mina, who can help me?*

I race out of our room and up the stairs.

"Have you seen Gabe?" I ask Anton. He's the first one I spot when I get back to the main part of the house. I really really hope Gabe isn't on a mail run right now.

"He's in the office."

I let out a relieved sigh. "Thanks."

I don't bother knocking when I reach the office. "Hey, I need your help."

Gabe looks up from his laptop. "What do you need?"

He is so hopelessly mope-y lately. He gallantly decided to leave Julie alone because she can't bring herself to submit to him and all his kinky desires. I mean, I get it with all her trauma. I was once her. So... I get it. And I don't even think she started out kinky—unlike me.

But now they're just... existing together or not really *together*, but you know, in the same general giant mansion. It's annoying the shit out of me.

"Ummm, it's really more of a show than a tell sort of situation. Could you come with me?"

He follows me back down to the dungeons, and into the bathroom.

"Mina, what the fuck happened? Is he all right?"

"He'll be fine, I dosed him with some of the drugs."

Gabe's eyes are the size of saucers. "You WHAT?"

I think he's genuinely afraid for my life right now, and that's sort of sweet. I've always had a soft spot for Gabe ever since he rescued me from Brian when Lindsay locked me in a cage when I first got to the house.

It was a long time before I knew it was Brian who set that situation up because he didn't like the idea of me trapped like that, but he also didn't want to kill off his sociopathic evil reputation in a single afternoon. So in the grand scheme of things, Brian was my real rescuer that day

Still, Gabe has always been kind to me. And he's been the only person at the house to not treat me like a total alien since I've changed.

"Oh my God, Gabe, if you knew how he was being, you would have dosed him, too. But I need your help moving him."

Gabe is probably the only trainer at the house who likes Brian at all. I like to think they have a weird sort of Bromance going on. At least I'm shipping them that way.

"He'll kill me."

"I mean, not if he's chained up," I say, batting my eyes sweetly. "Also, we did take care of your Dmitri problem. And I got all the girls to safety."

Gabe lets out a long sigh. "I'm telling you, he will kill me if he finds out I helped you do this."

"I doubt it. You're the closest thing to a friend he has and the only one who isn't constantly antagonizing him."

Gabe seems to think my faith in Brian is misplaced, but he picks him up under his arms anyway.

"Can you grab his feet?" he asks.

"Yes, I'm an expert at this part." Between Halloween night and the Dmitri job I could do workshops on this part.

"Where are we taking him?" he asks.

I pause to think.

"Mina, he's heavy. You don't even know where you're taking him?"

"Give me a second, I'm narrowing it down."

"Narrow faster."

"Okay, okay, cell A. It's the one right next door to our room."

"Thank you."

We lug Brian to cell A. Well, Gabe does all the actual lifting and lugging. I'm more like the person holding up the bride's train as she walks down the aisle. It's really more of an honorary position than an active role in lifting anything heavy. Though I do lift heavy in the gym... but not *Brian* heavy.

"Where?" Gabe asks.

"Ummm, let's chain him to the pole in the center."

"Are you sure it'll hold him? For your safety..."

"I'm sure. It's solid steel and concreted into the floor and ceiling. It's not coming up. We can secure him with the manacles coming down from the ceiling and out of the floor. We can let the pole take his weight."

"Are you sure you don't want to use a different piece of furniture?"

To Gabe's credit he doesn't ask what my actual plans for Brian are.

I thought about the St. Andrew's Cross, but that reminds me too much of Halloween and his request for punishment. I don't want it to look too much like that night. And any of the furniture he'd have to lay on would make him feel far too vulnerable, which might close him off more. And that's not the point here.

"I'm sure," I say.

Gabe helps me secure him, then lingers in the doorway.

"You planning to watch the show?" I ask

"Are you *sure* about this, Mina?"

"I mean, he saw me jabbing the syringe in his throat so it's really not like I have any plausible deniability here or any general safety after making that choice. It's safer to have him chained."

"But you've got to let him go sometime."

"I'll take my chances."

Gabe sighs. "Okay. Good luck."

And then I'm alone and second guessing every choice I've made today.

3
BRIAN

I feel groggy as I wake up, and it takes me a moment to remember where I was and what I was doing. But soon enough it all comes back and crystallizes in my brain. Mina, the syringe, the sharp pinch in my throat, and then the world taking a nap.

"Mina!" I shout, rattling the chains. I'm beginning to regret just how sturdy I made them.

The dungeon is filled with candles. The bare bulbs in the ceiling I usually use when I'm in here are off. The bulbs give off a serial killer vibe, but I have to admit, there is an artistry in the candlelit dungeon—a sophisticated eeriness that is pure Mina.

I try to twist my body around to see her, but she's either left me alone completely or she's in my one blind spot. Would she really leave me chained up alone and unconscious with fucking fire?

"Mina!"

"Calm down. I'm here."

Her voice is a quiet seductive purr coming from the dark corner directly behind me. There's a long beat of silence, and then she emerges from the shadows. Her boots click across the concrete floor as she moves toward me.

"You really are flirting with death now, aren't you?" I have no idea what would possess her to pull a stunt like this. "I tell you I almost killed you, and your response is to chain me up? Maybe you do have a death wish after all. Maybe you knew Gregor wasn't me all along. Is that it? Were you just looking for some strange? Wondering if all killers fucked the same? Or maybe you'd just gotten bored with me."

She's silent, refusing to take my bait, she just watches me with a devastating calm I know she learned from me.

I sigh. "I don't know what the fuck you're hoping to accomplish with this. You have to unchain me sometime."

"I know."

"And what do you imagine will happen when you do?"

She moves to stand in front of me, leaning down so that we're eye level as she holds my gaze in hers. "Well, I'm hoping you'll be Brian again."

"Be careful what you wish for."

I start to look away, but she grips my chin and forces my gaze back to hers, unwilling to allow me to escape inside myself.

"You listen to me. You can push me away and punish us both for bullshit that never happened, but I'm not giving up on you. You might be a psycho, but you're *my* psycho. I know who you are. I know *what* you are. And I'm not flinching from it. So the fact that you had some big emotions happen that got away from you... so fucking what? You didn't act on it."

I swallow hard around the lump forming in my throat, refusing to let her words affect me. How can she even look at me after what I admitted? Instead I go back to the logistical nightmare she's gotten herself into with my captivity and my worries about what my crazy side will do to her the second I'm free again.

"How did you even get me in here?" I know she can't lift me on her own. It means someone had to have helped her, and I have a feeling I know who.

"Gabe helped with transport."

I knew it. "I'll kill him."

She just smiles sweetly. "No you won't."

"And what exactly is your plan here, Killer?" I rattle my chains again, ignoring her supreme and misplaced confidence that I won't go after Gabe for his involvement in this.

"I'm rethinking your request from Halloween."

"It was stupid. You were right. Punishing me won't help anything."

She laughs at this. "What a convenient time for you to have this realization. But no, I'm not going to punish you, Brian, not in the way you're thinking. But I am going to lead for a while, until you find your way back to me."

I just stare at her because I need her to speak plainly instead of in these damned riddles and also because I'm trying not to feel the one million things she's making me feel right now. And the loudest thing isn't even rage, if my erection is any indication.

I haven't had an erection in her presence in nearly three weeks, since Halloween. It's not that I've somehow lost attraction for her. It would be impossible not to be attracted to Mina, but my body decided to put my desire on lockdown after Halloween, the shame of my dangerous thoughts dousing the flames for her safety.

I can't fuck her. She isn't safe with me.

For a few days we were busy dealing with Gabe's job, but once we were back and there was nothing in our dungeon room but me and Mina, I knew we were past fixing. I couldn't let myself want her anymore—not for even a moment.

Only now, when I can't act on these urges, does my body finally allow me this expression of desire.

I let out a hiss as she trails her fingertips lightly down my chest, over the abs I've worked so hard for, and then she's languidly stroking my cock.

"Mina, don't."

She stops and crosses her arms over her chest, then she starts to pace the cell. I can't help but watch and fully take her in. She's wearing a black leather miniskirt with a slit up the side—not that there's much fabric there to slit—fishnets, and thigh-high boots. A black leather corset with red ribbon lacing completes this look. Her dark chocolate brown hair is tied up in a high ponytail.

Finally she turns back to me. "Do you trust me?"

"Of course I trust you. It's not you I'm worried about."

She strides back over to me, and then her hand is caressing over my cock again.

"Mina..." I groan, willing myself to tell her to stop, but the words refuse to come.

"Look, I'm not dealing with your weird little guilt party anymore. It's fucking unnatural. You don't trust yourself? Fine. Then trust me."

"What exactly are you asking for?"

"I'm asking you to put yourself in my hands and trust me to drive for a while."

"What does that mean?"

"You know what it means. Don't play dumb. You've lived in this house far too long not to understand power exchange."

I just blink. I mean I am chained up here, and it's not as though we haven't had our games back and forth, but she wants something real. She wants my surrender to her. My *real* surrender. And it isn't a completely unfair ask. She's given me hers, after all.

"What are the parameters? What would this entail?" I don't know why I'm asking. It's crazy. I can't allow this to happen.

Even if she's the one holding the whip, it doesn't make her safe.

"Upstairs with the house, we continue as we have been. There's no reason for anyone up there to know our private business. For jobs, we continue as we've been—equal partners. Down here, privately? You're mine. I initiate, you comply. I give the orders; you obey them. Without questioning my methods or complaining."

"Mina... I don't see how this can..."

"Shhhh." She presses a finger against my lips. "You don't trust yourself. Trust me. I need you to commit to this. It's not forever, just until you trust yourself again."

"But I'm still stronger than you, even if you tie me up, you have to let me go eventually, what if..."

"You're not going to kill me. And if you misbehave like a bad puppy, well you have to sleep sometime, and I know where the drugs are. I'll punish you if you *actually* do something wrong."

I can't believe this, but I want to do it. I want to let go of the responsibility for just a little while—this tight leash I always feel like I have to keep on myself ever since I realized just how much danger I am to her.

If there is one person I trust in this world, it's Mina. I know she won't break me or hurt me. I know she won't humiliate me or treat me like some dog. But I don't know if I can. I'm afraid I'll slip the leash and bite her.

Several minutes pass in silence.

"Brian?"

I sigh. "Untie me. I can't do this."

"Brian..."

"Now!" I snap at her—like me snapping at her is going to make her feel motivated to let me roam free near her.

She's crying when she releases me from the shackles. As soon as I'm free, I practically flee from the dungeon. I want to comfort her. I want to hold her and kiss her and tell her everything's going to be okay, but I can't face her. I can't face myself. I go into our bedroom and put on a pair of pants and a black T-shirt. I can't go upstairs naked, and I'm always conscious of letting anyone at the house see the scars on my back from my childhood. I'm dressed and I'm about to ascend the stairs when her voice stops me.

"Brian!"

I freeze, my hand gripping the railing.

"A-are we over?"

I can't stand her tears. Why the fuck am I like this? Why can't I be a better man for her?

"I just need some space," I say quietly, still not able to look at her.

"All you've had is space. For weeks! Can't you see how this is killing me?"

I go to her and gather her in my arms and just hold her. "Please stop crying, Mina. I can't do what you want because I can't be intimate with you right now. I need some time to figure myself out. Please just give me that time."

She sobs against my neck, holding me so tightly as though I'm just going to throw her away or something. As though I don't want her.

"Shhhhh," I whisper against her hair. When she finally calms, I pull away from her, turn away, and go upstairs into the main house, praying she won't follow.

4
MINA

Another week passes with Brian avoiding me and me feeling like at any moment he's going to end things, since he obviously can't stand to be in the same room as me.

I'm finishing my burrito in the cafeteria when I feel the energy shift. I look up to find Brian blazing a path toward me, fury in his gaze.

"Come with me," he says when he reaches my table.

I've barely stood when he grabs my hand and half drags me past the lunch crowd. I know there are people in this room that fear for me right now and what Brian might do to me, but all I can think about is the electricity shooting through my body at his warm hand in mine. And besides, it's the first time he's touched me like this of his own volition in weeks. It's the most aggressive, dominant purely Brian energy I've gotten, and I don't care where it leads, I'm just glad it's back. It's so much better than self-recrimination Brian. That Brian gives me the ick. And I've been living in hell with that Brian for longer than I can stand.

As soon as we're in our dungeon room, he lets go of my hand and turns to face me. "We have to kill Dante."

"Dante Valentino?"

"How many other Dantes do you know?"

I breathe in his crackling angry energy. Killing isn't romance, but it's also not total avoidance. I'll take it.

I choose not to inform Brian that I actually went to high school with two guys named Dante. I'm sure he wouldn't appreciate it right now when he's buzzing with so much purpose.

He pulls a manilla folder out of the inside of his leather jacket, and starts putting things up on the murder wall with the clear thumbtacks already in place. The wall has been sadly blank since the Dmitri job ended.

"Why are we killing Dante?" I mean, not that I care, but I'm curious about this new and exciting intensity in Brian.

"That motherfucker let you go off with Gregor, and he *knew* it wasn't me."

I feel the rage emanating off him. It's like if he doesn't kill something right now he'll combust. God, if only he'd direct some of that passion at me.

I never mentioned Dante or our conversation from Halloween night. I wasn't keeping it from Brian or anything. I'd forgotten about it altogether until just now. So it never occurred to me that Dante knew Gregor was leading me off somewhere or that he was pretending to be talking to Brian so I'd let my guard down enough to be led away from the main party.

"How do you know that?" I ask.

He just turns and looks at me, his black eyes fathomless pits of evil, the clear urge for retribution simmering in their depths. I don't care what it says about me, I love this side of him. With Brian, vengeance feels like a delicacy—an indulgence I don't have to feel guilty for indulging in.

"Well, he was bragging about it for one thing and didn't

know I was nearby overhearing it. Also, he's pretty angry about Halloween. Apparently he considered Gregor a close friend—not just someone who did jobs for him. And so now, we have to kill him before he puts a hit out on... well, me, mostly. I don't think he's personally gunning for you. Gregor just had a sick vendetta which I don't believe Dante shares, but we can't be too careful. I fucking knew I should have just gone ahead and killed Valentino instead of sending him a message. He's not the kind of guy who takes messages very well. He's got too big of an ego."

I can't decide if I should try to calm Brian down or just let him burn off this anger. It's a good sign that he's letting me see his darker edges again. He's been handling me like glass, holding back, giving me all the Jekyll and none of the Hyde.

"Do you know when you want to do it?" I ask.

"Before Christmas. Dante is usually pretty quiet around this time of year. He's got a big Italian family, and they do a big Italian Christmas. I've never known him to work in December, but if he's harboring this grudge, you can bet he plans to take me out immediately after the new year, and I don't intend to give him the opportunity to make that happen. The question is... does anybody have the balls to take the contract once he sets it in motion?"

"Let's not find out," I say.

"My thinking exactly."

5
BRIAN

"Motherfucker!" I shout, causing gasps from several mothers and one disgruntled dad.

The boy that was sitting on my lap starts to cry, and Mina quickly removes him and takes him back to his mother.

"He peed on me!" I hiss, when she returns.

Mina stifles a laugh.

Wait, I should probably back up and set this scene properly. Finding a way directly in to Dante's organization to do proper recon has proven to be impossible. I overestimated my ability to get close enough to him to get what I need to plan a proper hit.

The chance encounter that officially put him on my kill list wasn't something easily repeated. I imagine there are a lot of people besides me who want Dante dead, and he's determined not to make it easy.

Almost every target has some sort of weak spot, or a way to take a job doing some menial task with the real intent to get close enough to take him out. But Dante is far too paranoid for that. He runs the kind of background checks on household staff that you would expect to see in a highly classified government job. And he knows my face.

If he hired through an agency and didn't pay attention—like most of these arrogant assholes do—I'd be in and out with another notch on my gun belt in an afternoon. But no, there's no escaping Valentino's hard scrutiny and endless layers and levels of security protection.

I wish I had access to Drake Windsor's inside guy, but with Windsor gone, so is the mole. And even if I could get to him, he probably wouldn't know anything. I'm sure he wouldn't have information about weeks worth of Dante's schedule. That's the kind of convenient set-up you only see in a movie.

So, Mina and I decided to try a back door. One of Valentino's close friends owns a department store and keeps a private office on site. We somehow thought the best opportunity to look into this guy's computer files would be if I were playing Santa for the holidays. Correction, Mina thought this. I think she just has a weird Santa kink.

This is like every bad holiday movie rolled into one, and it's a testament to how hard Dante is to get to that I've resorted to this slapstick comedy solution.

I hate this Santa suit, and the beard is itchy. If I break out in a rash I'm going to torture the motherfucker slowly before I kill him. Assuming I'm ever able to get the man in a room alone.

"Santa's going to take a little break, kids," Mina says, putting up a gold glitter sign.

Somehow despite my shouted expletive, these kids are still eager to tell me what they want for Christmas. They all groan in disappointment.

"We'll be back in fifteen minutes," My little elf says brightly.

She doesn't look like the classic Santa helper elf. Instead of pointy ears and hat and red and green, she's wearing gold and white and doesn't have a hat at all—pointy or otherwise. She looks more like a fairy, but it was what they had in the costume closet. I don't even want to think about who else has worn these costumes before us and how much or little they've been washed in between.

"You can take a quick shower and go change into a new Santa suit." She says. She leans down when she whispers these words, and I get lost in the view of her cleavage for several long seconds.

We've been at this for five days now, and I haven't had an opportunity to get into the office. I'm sure with him being so close to Dante that there will be some informational trail I can follow to find out Valentino's schedule and how Mina and I can coincidentally be in his path long enough for me to politely murder him.

"We should call this a bust and try a new strategy. I would so rather be Krampus right now," I say.

She presses a kiss to my forehead and the kids make "ooooooh" noises. And I'm sure they'll break out into the "Kissing in a tree" chant at any moment.

But I go.

I dutifully go back, take a quick shower, and change into a new Santa suit. The fact that there are so many Santa suits makes me wonder how many kids pee or puke on the Jolly Old Elf in any given holiday season. I don't want to find out.

When I return, I don't see Mina, but I sit in the big Santa chair anyway. It looks more like a candy throne. How the fuck did I get here? Where in my life did I go wrong?

A kid wanders up to me without Mina's guidance, and I startle when I realize it's Aidan. I work to school my features even though he can't see them behind the white beard. I look back in the crowd to find none other than Uncle Martin has brought him down to see Santa. I haven't had time to check in on the kid since Halloween. It makes me uncomfortable to realize this. Something could have happened to him, and I don't want to think about why I even care about that.

I should just let fate decide what happens to him and disengage from this unhealthy obsession I've developed.

He sits on my lap and tugs at my beard, clearly not a true believer. He is six after all. And given what he's been through in his short little life it's a miracle he just has mild skepticism.

"Ho, Ho, Ho," I say in a deep voice, paranoid this kid is going to remember me from the night I killed his dad. "And what do you want for Christmas, Aidan?"

I don't know what just came over me. It's dangerous to use this kid's name, but the way his eyes widen as he moves firmly back into the *Santa is Real I just knew it!* camp, makes it worth the risk.

"I want my mommy and daddy back," he says quietly.

And if I had a heart, it would break right now. This kid.

"I'm afraid Santa isn't in the business of miracles, kid. How about a new video game system?"

He looks disappointed but not surprised that I can't magically bring his parents back from the dead. "What about that angel? Can I have her?"

"What angel?"

Aidan points, and I follow his line of sight to Mina at the other end of the store. I suspect she saw the kid and vacated the area for fear he'd recognize her. Too late. She's standing under a spotlight in the lingerie department, and she really does look like an angel right now.

I have no idea what to say to this kid in response to his request. I mean, how would I even fit her under the tree? It takes everything in me not to petulantly state that No, she's *my* angel and Aidan can't have her.

"She protected me from the bad man a long time ago," he states very seriously.

Oh to live in an age of innocence where five months is "a long time ago." And I realize with sinking clarity, that I'm the bad man this angel protected him from. His memories are confused and muddled. After so much change and grief and trauma, he's misremembering that night. He's somehow conveniently forgotten Mina was shooting people, too. Or maybe he just never saw her until she was helping him. Maybe he was too focused on me and *my* carnage to notice her tiny ball of fury.

I imagine it would have made the night much less scary to think of her as an angel and not one of the bad guys, so he at least had one person on his side.

"I'm afraid I need her at my workshop so all the boys and girls get their presents in time. Can I get you something else?" I ask, sounding like I'm a Holiday waiter. "Isn't there anything else you'd like, something you haven't asked your Uncle for?"

Now I'm treading on very dangerous ice because there is every possibility that Aidan will excitedly tell his Uncle all about how much I seem to know about him. And for that reason, I'm retiring as Santa Claus just as soon as this kid is off my lap. We'll just have to find another way to our target—it's not like this was a winning strategy anyway.

He thinks for a few minutes, and some other kid that's way too old to be visiting Santa tells Aidan to hurry up. I glare at the kid in question, and he backs down.

"Well," Aidan says, "There is this one thing."

He goes on to describe to me a sort of magnetic dinosaur building kit.

"I'll see what I can do." I'm about to disengage and send him on his way when he looks up at me, his face turning very serious once again.

"I know you can't bring my parents back, but you're magic, right? You fly through the sky with reindeer, so can you tell them something for me?"

"Sure, Kid." I can't deny his request twice. And anyway, he's not going to know I don't have direct access to his parents or that I never delivered his message to the great beyond.

"Tell them I'm going to be okay, and they don't have to worry, and I hope they are doing okay, too."

I nod, not trusting my voice. He gets off my lap and inexplicably gives me a high five, then runs off back to his uncle. I have to say, he's coping remarkably well for only five months out from losing his dad. I expected we'd be in a much worse place right now. But then maybe it hasn't fully hit him yet. He's had a lot of changes the past few months.

With his aunt, he was just trying to avoid her rage. And then he got to move in with his favorite uncle, and the holiday season started. I'm betting he's just very distracted by all of it.

We haven't even begun to see the long term effects. I'm sure of that. It's not that I want him to turn into a criminal. No, that's not the truth. I do want him to turn into a criminal. I want to teach him everything I know someday.

But it's a foolish and misplaced dream for a family that can never be. And men like me don't get to have dreams like that. And the fact that I'd even want it is exactly the reason I'm not fit to be a father.

6

BRIAN

Electricity buzzes along the surface of my skin as I smile down with a maniacal evil clown grin at Julie, Gabe's girl. Only that's the problem. She *isn't* Gabe's girl. She wears no collar to protect her from me. She's fair game—fresh innocent meat for me to play with.

I've got her strapped down to a metal chair in one of my cells.

I sent Mina off to do some recon. I don't expect her to learn anything useful. We've hit a dead end with Dante without even the first clue about how to get close enough to remove him from the gene pool. But I sent her away because she might get in the way of... this. I know she wouldn't approve. I'm being a very bad puppy right now.

I lean down closer and sniff Julie's strawberries and cream shampoo. "I've waited so long for this," I whisper against her hair. "Since you rebuffed our boy, Gabe, I've been waiting for the right moment to... fix you."

You can't do this. She's broken like Mina was.

I squeeze my eyes shut to block out the stirrings of a long

dead conscience. I've already taken all the baby birds under my wing that I'm going to. Mina. Aidan. No more strays. No more.

I shove away a memory of Julie playing Chopin upstairs on the piano. I will not be soft with her. I will not spare her my rage. If Gabe wanted to protect her he should have locked a collar around her throat like he had some fucking sense. He knows the rules. Too many people around here are starting to think I'm housebroken, and I need to remind them of the monster that lives below.

She glances over at the metal tray table where I've laid out all my tools on white parchment. Her eyes widen as she realizes my plans for torture.

I place a hand on her knee. "You're trembling, Julie."

Minutes pass as she seems to be trying to come to terms with her fate, or else coming up with a plan for bargaining. Sex in trade for being spared? I don't think she's got it in her. She's far too sweet. If she can't even give herself to Gabe—the nice one— she certainly would never let my hands sully her.

"Please... don't do this... you can't. G-Gabe is my master."

I laugh. It's not a mere chuckle but the maniacal cackles of a mad man. Does she think I'm an idiot? I should punish her even harder for lying to me. "Oh, that's rich. Gabe is your master. I've seen no indication of that. You two don't even talk anymore. But clearly you know that's the only real protection from me—a collar around that pretty little throat that doesn't have my name on it. It's really the only deterrent I'll listen to. But you knew that. That's why you avoid me and try to stay in groups. It was a hell of a thing finding you alone with no witnesses around. Gabe is your master. That's adorable."

I pick up a metal nipple clamp and slowly and calmly start to unbutton her blouse. She seems dumbfounded that her attempt at magic words held no power over me. And I push back the voice in my head telling me not to hurt her, she's too much like

Mina. I can't cross this line. But I can't keep making exceptions. I can't keep losing pieces of myself to Mina's influence. I don't even know who I am anymore.

Finally Julie begins to struggle, pulling at her bonds. Her eyes are wild, and I just can't enjoy it like I usually do.

"Please! Please! Gabe is my master. I swear it." Her shrill words come out on choked sobs as the tears I would usually savor move down her cheeks.

I work to keep a sort of sarcastic amusement on my face because I cannot betray that this is actually affecting me. What is wrong with me? I nearly murder Mina, but I'm not sure if I can bring myself to hurt Julie? Everything is upside down.

I put the clamp back on the tray. "All right. Let's find out. You better pray he confirms your side of things. If he doesn't, nothing will stop me from the sadistic nightmare I will rain down upon you. And it will only be worse for this lie insulting my intelligence. Given these facts, do you want to alter your story?"

She shakes her head frantically.

I pull a phone from my pocket and click on Gabe's number from my contact list. "Gabe! It's your friendly resident psychopath," I say jovially.

"Yeah, you're just a big fluffy marshmallow," Gabe says.

I laugh. If only he knew. "Tell me, is Julie yours?"

"Your guess is as good as mine, man," he says, sounding both bitter and noncommittal.

"You know what I mean. Is she your slave? She tells me you're her master. She's begging and pleading and swearing to it so I won't hurt her. And I wanted to know if…"

"Don't touch her. I'll be there in five."

"Okay, very well." I end the call and put the phone on the metal table and sit back in the chair next to Julie's bound form. "He's coming down," I inform her.

She lets out a slow shuddering breath. She's shaken up, but

not as badly as I am. Gabe may get us both out of this performance art.

Less than five minutes go by and I feel, rather than hear, Gabe. I didn't bother to close and lock the door, so he's just hovering in the doorway. And he is pissed.

But not at me, it appears.

Julie starts crying again, realizing she still might be in some real danger since Gabe doesn't appear to be in a cuddly mood at the moment.

"Well, Gabe? Is she yours?"

He doesn't even look at me. He's too focused on her. I know they obviously aren't together. I feel the tension radiating off both of them. This isn't the scene of a couple reunited. It's pure ambivalence.

I swivel my chair to study my tools. "Okay, well, until somebody learns how to use their words, I'm going to play."

Julie flinches as I unbutton her shirt the rest of the way and pick up a small knife from the metal tray.

She panics and again begins to struggle. "Please," she whimpers. Her plea is directed at Gabe. If only she knew... I'm probably more likely to show her more mercy than he is right now. The kindest trainer in the house is having a hard sharp break with morality, and I've suddenly grown a heart.

I use the knife to slice open the front of her bra, then I put it back on the table and pick up the clamp. "Do you know how I know you aren't really his? I've known Gabe for a while now. If you were his, he never would have allowed you underwear."

I watch both of their reactions. Gabe looks at her for another second, and then turns away. Well, that's a plot twist I didn't see coming. I swallow hard around the lump forming in my throat. There's no way I can just let her walk out of here. Word will get around, and my entire fearful reputation will be destroyed in this house. I'm trying to think of something bad enough that I can do to keep the fear high, but mild enough not to completely break her.

"Master, please don't leave me with him!"

There it is... the magic word. Gabe stops, his body going rigid. He turns slowly. "Brian, release my property."

I put the clamp back down on the table and sigh. "If she's your property, where's her collar? How am I to know who is protected if they don't have a collar?" I don't know why I can't drop it. Maybe I just want these two crazy kids to end up together. Maybe I'm a twisted romantic at heart.

"It's being made," Gabe says.

"If it's not around her throat by the end of the week she's fair game."

"It will be."

"If she's your slave, why doesn't she act like it? Why don't I see any signs of it?"

"It's new."

Yeah. Like right now, new.

I start to unbuckle the straps binding her. "Hmmm, I'm still not convinced. Julie..."

Her gaze shifts to me. "Y-yes?"

"If you're really his slave and he's really your master, crawl over to him, kiss his boots like a proper slave, and thank him for his mercy."

I should just let her go and not tempt fate, but I want her to have a good story to tell of how she narrowly escaped the monster in the dungeon. I watch as she follows my order.

"Thank you, Master," she says gazing up at him from the floor.

"Stand up." Gabe practically growls the words at her.

I don't even know who he's mad at. I just got him the one thing he's wanted the whole time he's been moping about this stalemate. So it better not be me.

She stands and he takes her top the rest of the way off. I raise a brow at this. Am I about to get a live show? *Damn, boy. Didn't know you had it in you.* But much to my disappointment he only removes the bra and then puts her top back on.

I want to gloat about my correct assessment of his underwear rules, but I manage to keep this thought to myself.

"Brian is right about one thing. No underwear. Do you understand?"

I almost laugh out loud at this.

"Y-yes, Master."

"Let's go." Gabe's hand goes to her lower back as he guides her from the room.

"Oh Gabe?" I call after them.

"What is it?" Gabe says, his irritation clearly at the breaking point.

"You owe me a drink."

"For what?"

"I think you know for what."

He doesn't reply. I should at some point have a conversation with him about his role in helping Mina chain me up in the dungeon, but that would only call attention to the fact that I was chained up in the dungeon. Maybe it's best to let it go.

When they're gone I pick up my cell and dial another number.

"Hello, who is this?"

"I sent you an email with a photograph of a woman. Did you get it?" I ask, not bothering to give him a name.

"I'm sorry I'm not taking commissions right now."

"I think you will, Joseph. Or do you prefer the moniker, Quill?"

There's a long pause on the other side of the line. And finally he says, "Who is this?"

"Someone who knows you aren't dead, and that the entire art world would also love to know that little fact."

"What do you want?" he says, his rage barely restrained.

"You know what I want. The instructions are in the email."

"I do nudes, not pen and ink portraits. I'm not a street vendor. I'm a fucking artist."

"You're a fucking pretentious prick is what you are. Do the job, get paid, and keep your secrets. Or not. Your choice."

I disconnect the call before he can reply.

7
BRIAN

I'm sitting in the cafeteria, finishing up a plate of bacon and eggs when a piece of glossy paper floats down to the table in front of me.

"What's this?"

Mina sits across from me with a cup of coffee, a wicked gleam in her eyes. At this point we're just basically ignoring and avoiding the bad case of dead bed we've got. I haven't so much as kissed her since Halloween, but as long as we've got the distraction of a kill, we can both pretend everything isn't falling apart in slow motion. And we are great pretenders.

"You know how you said you'd rather be Krampus? Well... you're in luck... There's a Krampus Run, and guess who's going to be there?"

"You're kidding?" I glance down at the flyer with the date, time, and location, and already I can see the thrilling possibilities laid out before me.

"Wait, this is on Christmas Eve. Valentino doesn't go out on Christmas Eve. You must have gotten it wrong." Though I would love it if she hadn't.

"Nope," Mina says. "He's not doing the big family Christmas this year. There's a rumor he had a falling out with the family Matriarch, but no details were forthcoming. Nevertheless, he'll be there. He's on the list."

I want to ask what list, but I'm too pre-occupied with this idea that he would ditch his family holiday. So he just decided to dress up like Krampus instead? I'm sure there must be some sort of underworld business going on. It would be a great environment to hide in. It's the only reason someone like Valentino would participate in an event like this. So I feel immediately suspicious.

"Christmas Eve is a little late for a Krampus Run, don't you think?" I say. It's traditionally in early December.

She shrugs. "I'm not sure America fully *gets* Krampus yet. But points for effort, right?" She places a glossy gold business card with black embossed lettering in front of me.

I raise an eyebrow at the words *Benjamin Barker's Costuming Co.* in a sharp block font.

"We have to have appropriate costumes, otherwise they'll never believe we're supposed to be Krampus and we won't be allowed backstage at the event."

"We?" I ask.

"I mean, yeah. I'm totally dressing up, too. The bad news is, we're going to have to visit this guy in person and pay a lot of money, like... contract kill level money if we want him to rush us some costumes out in time."

Of course we do. "All right," I say with a sigh.

Mina squeals, drawing attention from several whispering women at nearby tables. "I'm so excited! I really felt like I got cheated on Halloween with all the formal evening wear and the fancy mask. You were the only one who got to wear a real scary costume."

My expression drops at this, not wanting to be reminded of the events of Halloween. I've been trying to just bury it. I can't believe she's joking around about it—like it's nothing. But she doesn't notice my shift in demeanor.

8

MINA

Benjamin Barker's Costume Company sits on the corner of Five Points. I have no idea what Five Points means, it's just what we've always called this part of the downtown. It's about six blocks away from *Dome*, Anton's spa, and about three from the Stryker Building.

I stare up at the skyline trying to imagine how this would all look with the top two floors gone. Would they have torn the whole building down, or just put up scaffolding and started repairs right away?

Brian nudges me. "You ready?"

"Yeah."

It's after sunset which only adds to the eerie feel of the place. A light jingle of bells rings out as we step inside the dimly lit shop. I almost walk straight into a hanging string of garlic bulbs but manage to see it in time and maneuver around.

"At least we've proven we aren't vampires," Brian says.

The shop has a sense of Carnival and Mardis Gras and the circus all rolled into one with heavy drapes in purple and gold and green. One of those old Zoltar fortune telling machines sits in the corner, clearly out of service, with its light still blinking. The old dark hardwood floors creak under our feet as we explore.

There's a glass counter case with shrunken heads inside, and I have no idea how that goes with "costuming." But here we are.

I get the sense that Benjamin deals more with people in professions that require costumes instead of children and adults on Halloween. Circus and carnival performers. Rock stars. Magicians. Theater people.

There are racks and racks of elaborate costumes that are clearly handmade—not mass produced in a poorly ventilated factory. As I stroke the thick fabrics, I realize they're made with real artistry and look like the kinds of costumes that could be used for movies.

There are rows of masks—also handmade—and accessories, and then an entire section of the store dedicated to magicians. Trick cards and flash paper and colorful handkerchiefs line one row. There's a gold sign that suggests making an appointment to see the private collection, which I assume is the more expensive professional magic equipment.

It may be hidden in part because it's so expensive, but maybe also to keep the tricks of the trade a secret from curious members of the public who might wander in off the street. With the Internet it's got to be harder than ever to do stage magic and wow the crowds.

I turn and nearly knock over a rack of white face makeup when I hear a voice.

"Can I help you?" I've never heard these words sound more sinister than they do in this moment as a tall middle-aged man with pale white face make-up and heavy black eyeliner emerges from a back room, through a bamboo curtain. A black cat jumps to the counter, curling her tail around her feet and glaring at us. We must have interrupted her sleep because she yawns dramatically then goes back to glaring.

"I heard you make Krampus costumes," Brian says, approaching the counter and dropping the gold business card on the glass as though it's a ticket to ride. The cat taps the card a few times with one paw then hisses at it.

Benjamin scratches the cat behind her ears, and she settles down. He raises a dark brow at Brian. It's a supervillain eyebrow, and I wonder if he's wearing a costume right now or if this is how his face really looks all the time.

"It's the first week of December, I'm afraid I don't have time to make any more Krampus costumes." He says this as though we are quite stupid to even make such a request.

"We just learned about the Krampus Run," I say, as though my lack of information will change his mind or how time works.

He sort of sneers at me then goes back to Brian, as if he's the kind of man who only speaks seriously and directly to other men.

"As I said, the costumes are quite ornate and require an enormous amount of work, and I'm not taking on any more private clients right now."

"I'll pay you half a million dollars," Brian says.

I work to keep my face blank. I did suggest to him that we might have to pay contract kill level dollars to get this done on such a short time crunch, but I didn't think he'd offer to drop half a million for it right out of the gate. I'm also a little insulted. I mean, he paid five million when he bought me. I don't think I fully realized until just now how willing Brian is to pay ridiculous amounts of money for things he wants without flinching.

As far as he's concerned, money is just a tool, and there's always more of it.

At this rate, Brian could just pay someone else to kill Dante and our problem is solved. But there's no way my guy won't take out his own trash. He wants to make sure it's done right. He's conscientious that way.

Benjamin just stares at Brian as though he didn't say

anything at all. He continues to pet the purring cat. Finally he blinks and says, "That's a very unusual offer, Mr..."

I tense, waiting to see if Brian is going to take the bait and offer this guy a name. Surely not.

"Sloan," Brian says. "Brian Sloan." Guess I was wrong about that.

He pulls a sharpie out of his pocket and flips over the business card to write down the number of his current burner phone. "This number will be good for a few weeks. Call me when it's done."

The proprietor looks back and forth from Brian to me and then back to Brian. I could swear some kind of recognition lit his eyes when Brian gave his name, and I don't like that at all.

He swallows hard and says, "Of course, Mr. Sloan. I can have the costume ready by the fifteenth."

Brian claps him on the side of the arm. "That's a good man. And, I need two. One for her." He nods in my direction.

Benjamin's gaze cuts briefly to me, and that sneer is almost back in place before he catches himself. "Of course. That shouldn't be a problem."

Brian turns to leave, and I follow him. Well, okay then. I admit I've never witnessed Brian do any sort of business deal with anyone, but this was... well, it was something. I'm a little turned on right now if we're being honest about it. I didn't expect his name to carry so much weight and power out in the world. How would this guy even know who he is?

"Oh, and Barker?" Brian says, pausing before reaching for the door handle.

"Y-yes, Mr. Sloan?"

"We weren't here. Remember, discretion is the better part of valor."

"Yes, of course. My lips are sealed." He does that weird motion of imaginary locking of his mouth and throwing away an invisible key, which causes the cat to jump off the counter looking for whatever she thinks he threw.

"I look forward to hearing from you," Brian says.

We're inside the car before I finally say "What was that all about?"

"What do you mean? I was getting our Krampus costumes. I thought that was what we were doing here."

"I mean... but you totally Renfielded him."

He turns in his seat to stare at me. "I what?"

"You know... Dracula's butt monkey... you completely hypnotized him or something."

Brian chuckles. "Don't be ridiculous, Mina. You think a guy like that doesn't deal with some unsavory types? My name is known in the underworld around here. And after the calling card I left on Halloween night, the fear of the name Sloan has never been higher."

I find this almost unbearably hot, but I don't say anything. I couldn't handle it if he pushed me away again.

When Brian checks the rearview mirror for traffic, I say, "Oh, and how is it that you can just run around telling people your full name like they aren't going to talk and the police won't show up at your door?"

He looks at me for nearly a full minute. And just when I think he isn't going to answer, he says, "In the first place, nobody knows where I live, and I'm careful to keep it that way. Also, Brian Sloan isn't my real name."

What?!

But Brian—or whoever he is—just maneuvers the car into the flow of traffic as if he didn't just pull the pin out of that grenade.

9

MINA

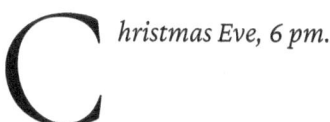

hristmas Eve, 6 pm.

I'm dressed in my normal black murder wear and strapped down with weapons. I've successfully fit my Krampus costume into a large black duffle bag, except for the mask, of course. It's too large and ornate to stuff into a bag. I'll have to carry it separately.

Also inside the bag are two whips. One is meant for the actual Krampus run—a flogger that can easily be used on people at the event without inflicting real damage.

We got Benjamin to put us on the official Krampus run list under false names along with photos of the costumes and masks we'll be wearing so we can get in to the staging area of the event.

The family-friendly Krampus parade is going on right now, but by the time we get there, it'll be the after-hours adult version where everyone in our path is fair game for chasing and whipping.

The rules of the run have been formally announced every-where so that all attendees know if they don't want to get hit, they'd better be off the street by nine o'clock. When the down-town countdown clock hits zero and the heavier industrial music starts playing, no one is safe.

These terms have been clearly stated everywhere: In the newspaper, on the website, on the local television news, and on large white signs with red letters clearly posted around the event. This is to protect the city from lawsuits, so no one can come out later and say they didn't know what was going to happen, claim abuse, and sue the city. I'm not entirely confident it will matter if some Puritan gets a bug up their ass, though. I'm feeling definite Purge Vibes around this event—or maybe it's just because that's what Brian and I are using it for... to purge Dante Valentino from this earth before he decides he wants to do the same to us.

The other whip in my bag is a short single-tailed whip with heavy pieces of metal and glass embedded into it. Brian has one as well. We'll pull these out once we've cornered Dante. I've still got to grab some dinner upstairs in the cafeteria. I carefully close the door to our dungeon room.

I'm only halfway down the hall when Brian comes down the stairs, and I nearly jump out of my skin. He wears what looks like layers and layers of rags and fur. He has an incredibly intricate demon mask with fur-hair in the back that matches the fur on the rest of the costume. The mask also features huge curled horns and glowing red eyes.

It would be scary enough all by itself, but Brian's cold dark energy spills out of it, rolling like a rushing wave toward me as he advances.

I take several involuntary steps backward, until my back is pressed flat against the door I just shut. He continues to quietly advance, making a big show of looking me up and down like I'm a meal he's ready to devour.

I'm trying so hard not to have a flashback to Halloween night. I thought I was over that—not what happened in the pumpkin patch, but the running, thinking I was about to be the next thing he cut up with that chainsaw.

I'm not really sure what it is with Brian and scary costumes, but I'm not sure he can handle them. It's like the power to hide behind a mask is just too much for him to switch off. Even though he has no conscience with most people, masks seem to take it to another level as he fully commits to the role of psycho killer or demon.

"Brian..." I say. I don't know if it's a warning or pleading.

He doesn't answer me. Instead he moves closer into my space, his hands on the door, framing either side of my body. He leans in close and sniffs me, even though I know he probably can't smell my perfume through his mask.

Except for sleep, we haven't been this physically close since Halloween.

"Run," he snarls next to my ear.

I know what he's doing. He's recreating the night we met and my foolish trip downstairs to the dungeons. But why?

When I hesitate, unsure if I should say no or play along, he drops one hand from the door and uses it to stroke the side of my face. It takes everything inside me not to start crying at the relief of his hand on me again. It's been so long, I'd forgotten what it felt like to enjoy the benefit of his full focused intensity.

He is so gentle right now, and I let out a shuddering sigh at the feather light touch. His caress drifts down my throat, his fingers pausing to feel my fluttering pulse as though he needs to catalog the evidence of what he's doing to my heart right now.

Then he strokes my breast, moving with aching slowness down my body as I arch into his touch begging for just a little more contact. I let out a strangled moan when he frees the button of my leather pants and slips his hand inside my panties, finding the damning evidence of my arousal coating his fingers.

"Run," he says again, his voice going even lower.

I swallow hard and take a deep breath. I'd be running up to the safety of the well-lit cafeteria. And I have to remind myself he isn't high from a fresh kill or in some heightened crazy state after finding me kissing someone else, however innocently.

He steps aside and even though I can't see his eyes behind the glowing red lights, I feel him watching me... and waiting. My hands shake as I button up my pants, and then I run down the hallway and up the stairs.

Adrenaline and arousal war within me. The first time we danced this dance he didn't chase me, but I know he will this time. It's the entire point of his demand.

I hear the cowbells jingling as he pursues me. When I reach the cafeteria, I keep running until I get to the buffet line. The girls look up from their meals, surprised to see me running, and then the bells announce Brian's arrival, and they understand why.

He's got his whip out—the safe one, not the murder one. And an electric thrill goes through me as I wonder if he's going to whip me right here in front of everyone. I feel my wetness increasing at that thought. I am a sick sick puppy. But it has been far too long since I enjoyed the decadent pleasures of his barely restrained darkness.

"Finally, someone's in trouble," I hear one of the girl's say, not bothering to hide her contempt for me. And I know Brian heard it too. His head jerks sharply in the direction of the woman who spoke. She's smart enough to get up from her chair but dumb enough to run from him.

It only excites him.

He chases her out of the cafeteria, the flogger snapping at her legs. I'm pretty certain this was not how anyone thought Christmas Eve dinner would go down at the house. And I know he's hitting her hard—much harder than a normal Krampus interaction. But then, he's Brian. And even though this is the "safe whip" is any implement truly safe in his hands?

She's shrieking and crying as she runs. I hear her echoing screams down the hallway, but I can't see what's going on or if Brian has pursued her and locked her in one of the main level rooms. Judging from the direction they went, I'd bet he'd choose the game room. He's tied me down to that pool table more than once in the middle of the night when everyone was asleep. My thighs clench at the memory of how he'd take one of the balls from the table and massage my drenched pussy with it until I begged him to fuck me.

But if Brian ties this girl down, it won't be to tease orgasms from her.

Before I can wonder if I should go after him to try to calm him down and refocus him back on our larger mission, he returns. By this point all Christmas Eve ham has been abandoned, and everyone is standing, in case they need to flee the scene.

Good instincts. Or maybe just garden variety common sense. They scatter like bowling pins as Brian barrels toward them, snapping the flogger at anyone he can get close enough to.

He chases them all out until it's just me and him remaining in the cafeteria. He picks up a piece of ham off one of the abandoned plates and it disappears under the mask. And then his attention turns sharply back to me, the glowing red eyes seeming to burn into me like embers straight from hell.

My heart beats wildly in my chest, but I don't run. A flogger isn't a chainsaw, after all. And unlike Halloween night I have enough presence of mind to understand the foolishness of running from this man. Instead I remain where I am, my hands gripping the metal bars behind me on the counter that the girls slide their trays across while getting their meals.

It's a really sturdy structure with an angled glass divider to shield the food. Obviously nobody official comes in to inspect this place for food safety standards, but everything is still industrial grade and up to code.

"Take your pants off."

Brian's voice is little more than a growl. He has fully committed to this role. I'm not sure my desire for him has ever been higher than in this moment. And I don't care what he does to me as long as his hands are on me.

I take my boots off first—it's the only way the pants can come off. Then I unbutton and slide out of the leather.

"Panties," he growls as he stalks closer.

I dutifully remove the scrap of red silk. He picks me up and sits me on the metal counter. It's sturdy enough to easily take a person's weight.

"Spread your legs."

"Brian, we're on a schedule. This may be our only shot at Dante." *Shut up. Shut up. Shut up. What are you doing, Mina? Just let this man do anything he wants.*

"I'm well aware of what time it is."

I take a deep breath and spread my legs giving him a full lewd view of my bare pussy.

"Lean back and get comfortable."

I do as he says, my back pressed against the glass, warm from the steam rising up off the food in the food warmers.

"Good girl."

It's been a long time since he's said these words to me, and I'd be lying if I said they didn't still have the power to affect me.

My breath stutters out as he fondles me now without any obstructions. I moan when his fingers dip inside me to feel how shamefully wet I am. What part of this gets me going? The danger? The terrifying demon costume? The openness of the space? The women of the house who I notice have snuck back to the fringes of the room and are now watching us from the shadows? The display of clearing the cafeteria to do whatever this is?

All of it? Maybe it's the kernel of my Brian returning to me— that dark dangerous edge he thinks I just tolerate instead of actually love. He thinks I love him in spite of his darkness—like I just make allowances for who he is, instead of embracing all of him.

He doesn't trust my declarations of love.

He flips the flogger around, and I gasp at the unexpected intrusion of the smooth polished walnut handle pushing inside me. My hips arch up to meet his endless punishing thrusts.

"You like being penetrated by a demon, don't you?" His voice is harsh and guttural.

"Y-yes," I gasp as my hips rise again to meet the friction of the flogger handle.

"Yes. *What*?" he demands.

"Yes, Master."

"Exactly. You're going to come hard for me and our audience like a good girl, aren't you?"

"Y-yes, Master."

So he *does* know they're watching. Maybe he heard them. Maybe he saw flashes of scurried movement. They are like animals waiting for a predator to leave so they can eat the scavenged remains. And all their dinners are getting cold as they wait and voyeuristically consume this spectacle instead.

He pumps faster and harder as the movements of my hips become more erratic and my vocalizations louder, wilder, more uninhibited. I don't know if I'm letting go or performing for our audience—or if I'm performing for Brian. I feel his satisfied smile behind the mask, even if I can't see it. So loud and intense is his energy projected at me.

I finally shudder as I come against the handle of the flogger. He allows me to convulse around it... waits for every flutter of my pleasure to play out like the long haunting strains of a violin. Then he removes it and holds it up to me, and I lick it clean like the good girl I am.

"You filthy, filthy girl," he says. "I'm going to be beating people with this tonight. What would the good people of our small metropolis have to say about that do you think?"

I start to get up, but he holds me in place. "Stay. Don't close your legs. I want to look at you like that."

I nod, and when he's sure I won't move, he goes around the counter to fix a plate of food and a glass of iced tea. Brian returns to me with a tray and places it on the counter.

He proceeds to take his time feeding me, all while I know the girls of the house are too afraid to come in here and disturb him in order to finish their own dinners.

His message is very clear. The alpha wolf eats first. I may be his, but I am not theirs. I'm not "just some slut" at the house. He cares for me, and they'd better put away their drama, fall in line, and accept it. Because as far as the women of this house are concerned, I am the alpha wolf.

"What about you?" I say after the plate is clean. And I don't know if I mean what about his sexual needs or needs for food.

"I ate before I put the costume on. I'm going to go downstairs and get cleaned up. Be ready to go in twenty."

He leaves me and descends back down the stairs to the dungeons. Once he's gone, the other girls timidly return to the room and their food. They can't even look at me. They're jealous, angry, embarrassed, but I'd lay good odds this weird power struggle between me and them that has been bubbling up since my return from Japan has finally come to its conclusion.

———

Both Brian and I are dressed normally as he drives us to the venue. He hasn't said a word about what happened in the cafeteria, and I don't think he's going to. I don't know if this is an indication of the shift back to normalcy for us or if he was only able to do all that because he could hide from me inside a character.

I'm not sure how I feel about that, but I know right now we have to be focused on the kill. Whatever our remaining interpersonal hiccups, they'll have to be dealt with at another time.

He parks the car at the back of a large gravel lot not that far away from where we parked on the Fourth of July. We put our Krampus costumes on over our clothes and hide our more deadly whips under the thick layers of fabric and fur.

And of course we have other weapons... knives and guns, just in case. I don't think we can use the guns, but we have them. This event is sponsored by the city and is crawling with police which is part of why it makes it so insane for us to take out Dante here. In public. But it also makes it unexpected.

Valentino is unlikely to have heavy guard around him in this environment when he thinks his identity is shielded so fully from his enemies.

It's cold outside, but the heavy layers make the ambient air feel comfortable. Brian got a peek at the Krampus list when he picked up our costumes and took a photo on his phone of what Dante's costume looks like. I studied it for most of the drive to lock specific details into my memory. We've got about an hour before the run starts, and I hope it's enough time to find our target.

It's a four block walk to the staging area from the car. Brian gives our fake names, and a member of the security team scans the list and checks our costumes against the photos, then he nods and waves us in.

There's no sign of Dante in the staging area. I knew there probably wouldn't be. After all, most of the Krampus demons are out in the parade working the crowd. We follow a roped off area until we're on the main road that's supposed to be reserved for the participants in the parade.

A live band on a nearby stage plays holiday classics with an uptempo rock twist as kids get their pictures taken with one of many Krampus demons as they parade down main street, ringing bells and waving to the assembled crowd.

Some of the children cry and hide behind their parents at the scary demon masks. It's especially endearing when a little girl being held by a Krampus seems to realize the terrifying thing holding her and starts sobbing. He bounces her on his hip to calm her down.

Most of the kids seem to be more fascinated than scared of the Krampus demons. Given my short experience as a Christmas elf, I'd say shockingly Santa gets more tears—or maybe that's just Brian.

But no, a small boy runs up to us and hugs Brian around the legs, causing him to leap back in surprise.

"This one! I want to get my picture made with this one!" he shouts. He can't be more than four.

"I'm sorry," the mother says, juggling a bag and her phone.

Brian just nods and stands still for the photo.

"Thank you," the woman says after snapping the picture and grabbing her little boy's hand to take him back to the parade line.

A giant clock over the stage counts down with a red LED display and a loud ticking sound that can be heard faintly even over the live music, reminding everyone that the family friendly part of the event is about to wind down.

"Is Dante in the parade?" I ask, leaning close so Brian can hear me above the crowd.

"I don't know. Come on." He grabs my hand and we wind through the people and demons until we finally spot our target.

Valentino wears an especially elaborate mask, and I can tell Benjamin had the time to carve more intricate horns. He waves and tosses candy into the crowd. We fall in line just behind him, shadowing his movements.

The procession goes down three blocks, then circles back around to where it started. We stay close to Valentino the entire time. I feel the adrenaline buzzing through me, excited over the fact that Dante has no fucking clue his killers are marching next to him in a parade, and that this is the last thing he will ever do in life.

I hope he enjoys himself, this last fleeting feeling of freedom —this one night without bodyguards that proves to be his fatal mistake. Brian confirmed that Dante is without an entourage tonight when he checked the list. Every single Krampus is accounted for on that list, and none of them are Dante's men. He foolishly came alone.

His alias, Frederick Valentine is known to Brian. Maybe Dante thinks he's slicker than he really is. Or he didn't expect anyone to find out he was skipping out on his family's traditional Christmas Eve gathering—something so out of character for him.

The band stops playing, and the clock gets louder. I glance up to find only a minute left before the event switches tracks entirely. I've been so focused on us not losing sight of our target that I didn't notice the energetic shift in the air.

I look around to find no children left. Police are moving through the crowds, ID'ing anyone who looks suspiciously underage.

I lean in closer to Brian. "Are you sure we can pull this off?"

I'm nervous about the police presence here. This is so unbelievably risky.

He squeezes my hand in response and reassurance. I take a deep breath as a buzzer sounds. The new band starts playing hard industrial rock. And then the running and screaming begins.

Brian and I both pull out our "safe" whips and shadow Valentino as we chase people in the close-by vicinity of those he's chasing. Our whips crack at people's legs. Shrieks, screams, and giggles fill the space, nearly drowned out by the music.

Brian is staying more aware of Dante, while I keep my focus on the cops. We have to wait until they're distracted, until they've moved to another area of the event. It's all rather predictable. The running, the chasing, most of the people moving in a pattern very similar to the three-block parade track we just walked.

The police keep pace with the bulk of the crowd where they think the danger of real violence breaking out is. And yet, we are the true danger here.

Finally, we have our moment. Brian signals to me, and I nod. We both switch from the safe whips to our kill whips. We bump and herd Dante away from the crowd, back toward the noise of the stage.

"Hey! What the fuck!" Valentino shouts, but it sounds like a whispered growl underneath the music—as though it could be just a growling backup vocal to the band on stage.

We work as a unit to rip at his costume, so we can get to vulnerable unprotected skin. He didn't wear an entire separate set of clothes under his heavy costume, and because it is a costume, buttons and zippers pop free much more easily than they should.

He struggles and runs from us, but he only ends up getting entangled in cords and stage equipment. He trips and falls in a tangle, and then in concert with Brian, I allow that terrifying part of me to come out—my own monster that mirrors his—and we beat Dante to death while his screams blend into the music and the screams of the other event participants.

It's only after it's done that Brian removes his mask to confirm for sure that it's him. There's something unsatisfying in our victim not knowing it was us—or why. But I feel Brian's buzzy adrenaline—the same frenetic energy from Halloween. Only this time when he turns toward me, I don't run from him.

But I sense the shift, like maybe this is the moment he'll come fully back to me. Even behind the costume... maybe we'll have a repeat of the pumpkin patch—a night I have shamefully fantasized about on an obsessive loop for weeks now. I've brought myself to orgasm under the spray of the shower more times than I can count, thinking about that night.

And the most shameful part is that my fantasy never starts with the fucking. It starts with the chase. Brian is right... I don't have a death wish but I do flirt with death. How could I not, when I sleep with the reaper every night?

We're about to make our exit when two new Krampus demons pop out from around the side of the stage. Their gazes shift to Dante's fallen body then slide slowly back to us. They're too close to allow us to run.

Everything is so loud, and with the masks I can't communicate effectively with Brian to know what to do. Who are these people? Are they just curious participants who stumbled upon a murder scene? Are they undercover cops? Are they men with Dante that we simply missed because they weren't the usual suspects?

I drop my whip and grab one of my knives. I keep it concealed under the layers of my costume, finally jabbing it in and upward under the ribs of the Krampus demon who rushes me. He doesn't see the glint of metal until it's too late. I can't tell what Brian is doing from this angle, but he seems to be scuffling with the other guy.

He's got the guy's mask off now and is interrogating him— demanding information now that he's got the upper hand in the fight. I scan the area, looking for cops or witnesses to our crimes. Was Dante worth it? Are we going to get out of this? My hands drip with the blood of the man I just killed, his body sprawled at my feet, while Brian continues to yell at the other one.

The run is circling back around as the Krampus demons herd their prey back toward the stage. We're too exposed here. Too visible. Somehow we've managed to move closer to the side of the stage, closer to the visibility of the crowd that doesn't realize what's happening around them. They're too taken with the event. They're too concerned with taunting or fleeing pretend demons with whips to notice the real monsters of the night.

The screams of the crowd mix in and cover up the scream of Brian's victim as he hits the ground. The cops are still at the back of the crowd, but they're making their way closer. They'll see us soon enough if we don't get the fuck out of here.

Just as I'm about to run for Brian and grab his hand, I feel a hard grip on each of my arms, and for a moment my heart drops in my stomach, and I think it's cops, and we're about to be arrested and lose everything. We're about to be separated forever.

"Brian! Run!" I scream. If I'm about to be taken in, at least he can save himself.

He turns glowing red eyes back toward me, and suddenly he's not fucking around. He rushes us, pulls out a gun from under his costume and puts two bullets first in one man and then in the other.

They release me and are on the ground before I even realize they weren't cops at all, but other Krampus demons. The gun fire draws attention as people scream and scatter and the band stops playing. Brian grabs my hand and we run in concert with the fleeing crowd, blending into their panic to escape into the night.

10

BRIAN

Mina and I blend into the crowd, making our exit as the shrieks of horror rise up, separating themselves from the screams of people just having fun running from holiday demons—as people begin to realize they've stumbled upon actual dead bodies and not just a macabre Krampus display.

When we've separated off from the crowd, we run the few blocks to the Stryker building. I'm grateful I still remember the code and that Martin hasn't bothered to change it. Why would he? He has no reason to suspect anyone has ever breeched his security or that anyone has ever died in this building. The cleaners were very meticulous that night.

Once inside, we shed our costumes, clean the blood off us in one of the bathrooms, and get on the elevator to ride to the top. Mina is shaking from the huge adrenaline dump she just experienced, and I'm not faring much better. I pull her against me, and hold her until she calms.

This was entirely too stupid of a mission. I was just so desperate to get to Valentino, but I never should have tried to pull off a kill in such an uncontrolled environment with so many potential witnesses. Masks don't make us invincible from capture.

"Who were those guys?" Mina asks finally when we reach the top floor. "Were they with Dante?"

I shake my head, remembering the small amount of information I could get out of one of our attackers before I had to put him down. "He said Benjamin Barker told him we'd be there and showed them what our costumes looked like."

"But why?"

"I don't know. Someone with a vendetta? Someone hired by someone with a vendetta thinking they could get the drop on us, the same way we were doing with Valentino?"

"Did Dante know we were coming, then?"

I shake my head. "I don't know, but we're going to fucking find out."

It all happened far too fast. I rack my brain trying to figure out who might be waiting in the wings to take me out. Maybe my Halloween display was more foolish than I originally anticipated. Instead of striking fear, it seems to have riled up some enemies.

We set up in Martin's office, and I dig through his desk drawers. He hasn't changed this office since his brother's death, and Stryker kept binoculars to get a good view of the street.

When I find them Mina and I take turns using them to watch as the crime scene is cleared and taped off with yellow caution tape—as ambulances and police fill the night with sirens and lights. A television that Martin set up in the office gives us access to a surprisingly prompt live newscast. But then again, the local media was already on site for the event. The news interrupts what were probably happy and heartwarming Christmas movies.

"Just hours before Santa's expected arrival in the homes of

children all across the city, a brutal massacre has taken place at the downtown Krampus run, with a startling five victims, one beaten to death, two stabbed, and two shot." the blonde newscaster says.

We already have a scary killer name... or at least one of us does. The words: "Yuletide Slayer at large" scroll and flash across the bottom of the screen. The Mayor arrives at a podium to the click of flashing cameras and says some horrified but somber words which were probably hurriedly scribbled from the back of his limo.

Speculations are made about if the killings were personal or some random psychopath. Questions are taken from the crowd. Citizens are interviewed one by one.

When interviewed by the reporter on camera, one older woman says, "Well, this is what happens when you invite the devil into the Lord's holiday. I still have Midnight Mass to attend in the middle of all of this."

She's clearly not one to let her apparent trauma get in the way of her duties to the Church.

I'm curious if anyone will inform her of the long history of Krampus runs in Europe, many sponsored by the Church. I also wonder how this sanctimonious cow just happened to be here to be interviewed in the first place if she thinks it's all so evil. The nearest church is two miles away. What would have prompted her to even attend this debauched BDSM-lite social function? I have doubts we'll be seeing another Krampus run here any time soon, so she needn't worry herself about future invitations to the devil.

I wander down the hallway to a break room and find some microwave dinners in the freezer. I heat a couple up for me and Mina and take them back to the office along with some canned drinks.

"Hungry?" I ask.

She looks up from the television and nods.

"It's nothing fancy."

"Don't be silly, I love cardboard lasagna," she says, fighting to keep her face serious.

I just smirk in reply, glad she seems to be back to herself.

I want to lay her out across this desk and fuck her brains out, but I still don't trust myself.

I peel back the plastic film on my food and sit on the office sofa to eat. "I'm sorry we've got to be holed up here for a few hours."

"It's fine."

I can tell she wants to say something else, and I wonder if it's about what happened tonight at the Krampus run or what happened before all of that in the cafeteria. I don't know if I've ever felt this uncomfortable around her in the entire time I've known her. I feel like a teenager on an awkward first date, and it takes everything in me not to say something completely inane.

"I thought it would just be Dante, and we could slip off," I say, stupidly.

"I know." She's still watching the newscast, barely paying attention to her food as she eats.

I didn't think we'd be jumped or that Benjamin would be so stupid as to disobey my direct order. He's got to be eliminated. He's a loose end now, and if he couldn't keep his mouth shut in such a small matter as our attendance to the event, then he'll definitely talk to the police.

So far it doesn't appear the authorities yet know they'll need to talk to the one person who was responsible for all the Krampus costumes—the one who knew every person who would be at the event tonight. I don't think they even yet realize that there is a single point of contact for all these costumes... Or in me and Mina's case, a single point of failure—the one man who stands between us and jail cells. This middle-aged goth punk won't be the one who separates me from her. I fucking vow it.

The Krampus demons will be the primary suspect list, and I can't risk that Benjamin might have more details on his than the list the security guard had with only our fake names and costumes.

After she eats, Mina angles the TV toward the couch, turns the volume up, and then comes to snuggle with me. I put an arm around her as she burrows against my chest like a small forest creature.

"I'm going to take a nap. Wake me when it's time to take care of Benji."

I smile softly. I didn't even have to tell her why we were waiting or why we had to come here instead of just going home. That's my girl.

I continue to watch the footage until it winds down and the cameras shut off. The screen goes back to the Christmas movie as if nothing untoward happened at all. I watch out the window until the flashing lights finally fade away, and the street is dark. I press a kiss to the top of Mina's forehead and let her sleep for another half hour. She needs the rest.

11

BRIAN

It's after one o'clock in the morning. Benjamin's Costume Company has been closed for hours. If there are any unsatisfied customers, they'll have to make their complaints after the holiday.

The only trouble is, dead men don't give refunds. Though I'm pretty sure all sales were final anyway. I pick the lock, and the bell jingles to announce our presence. The only light in the place comes from the perpetually malfunctioning Zoltar machine and the purple lights in the glass counter, eerily illuminating the shrunken heads.

I almost walk right into the hanging string of garlic and Mina giggles behind me. It's not just a prop, it's fresh, so I wonder if Barker is a superstitious man.

He has a black cat so he can't be too superstitious. The cat sits on a nearby bookshelf and hisses down at us. I'm surprised there isn't a security system, but I casually cased the shop the last time we were here, and there were no signs of one—no little boxes to input a code. Unless it's in the back away from prying eyes. But it would be quite a jog to get to it in time before the alarm went off.

So I'm going with the theory that there's no electronic security system in this building—just a lock nearly any dumb teenager with a lock-picking kit and access to the internet for a quick tutorial can get into. Maybe he doesn't worry that a lot of people want to steal from his shop. If he keeps the money locked away somewhere else... It isn't as though there's a huge black market for shrunken heads and clown makeup.

Not only is there garlic, but there are sigils hanging near the door and cash register, something I didn't take notice of in previous visits. Does he believe magic will stop intruders? Is he a believer in magic in general? He lives in an apartment just above the shop, and before I can wonder if we're going to have to break in to that, too—and if maybe that's where the real security is—a bleary-eyed Benjamin minus his goth makeup comes downstairs into the main shop. He pushes aside the bamboo curtain. The cat jumps up onto the counter to be closer to him and continues to glare at us.

We're back in our Krampus costumes—I don't know why. It just felt like the creepy thing to do. Or maybe it's a form of cover in case a stray witness still lurks nearby. Benjamin is barely awake and doesn't seem to have registered the danger we present.

I had thought since he has enough dealings with the underbelly of the city and since my name actually meant something to him, that he would have the good sense and wisdom to keep his mouth shut, but you just can't trust normies. And clearly his loyalties were already to someone else despite my reputation. I knew it was a risk giving my name—but I also knew it was the quickest route to gaining his compliance and gaining access to Valentino at the critical moment.

"C-can I help you?" he asks.

"You had one job, Benjamin," I say, as though I'm a parent who is deeply disappointed in his conduct.

He recognizes my voice, even muffled behind the Krampus mask. His eyes widen and he turns to run, but I jump the counter and stop him, pushing him into the back room, and pressing him against the wall.

Back here, it's clear he *does* believe in magic—its protective power, its darker powers. There are more sigils back here as well as candles and tarot cards spread out, and carved stone idols on a nearby shelf representing what are probably deities he prays to. Or maybe ancestors or guardian spirits. I'm not so much into the occult. I just know it looks spooky and would make a good set for a TV show centered around witchcraft. But I'm a normie in his world as much as he is one in mine.

Let's find out which one of us has the real power.

I grip Benjamin's throat hard. "What did you say to Dante?"

"W-who's Dante?" He chokes out.

I squeeze harder until his face goes red from it, and then release him to let him gasp and choke and cough, as he tries to get back to the familiar safety of sweet oxygen.

"Tell me," I growl. "Don't play fucking games. I was told that you told someone we would be there. Was it Dante?"

Benjamin holds up his hands defensively as if he knows I'm not going to like what he has to say next. "I-I don't know who Dante is. I swear. T-there was a guy who was looking for you, and I told him you'd be there."

"How about Frederick Valentine? Does that name mean anything to you?"

Recognition slowly dawns in his eyes. "Y-yes, he bought a costume for the event. But I d-don't know him. That's not who I talked to."

I'm not sure if I believe him. "If you want to survive this

night, you will tell me the truth. Did you talk to Dante Valentino?"

"N-no! I don't know him! I told you!"

"What about the guy you talked to? Who is he?"

"I-I don't know... he came in for a costume. I don't know him. He just mentioned he was looking for you and asked if you were going to the event."

I wonder if it was some kind of set-up. Was Dante looking for me? Or was it truly someone else?

"P-please... I'm sorry. I didn't think. I just thought he was a f-friend of yours."

"Never met the guy," I say.

"S-so I told you what you wanted to know, so w-we're done here, right? I-I can go back to my apartment?"

"Brian..." Mina says, putting a hand on my arm. "Let's just go. He didn't mean to..."

I shake my head. "You believe that, Mina? Really?" I can't trust this guy. He'll talk to the cops. He's too scared. He's too unreliable. He will absolutely name us for this crime because he'll think me being behind bars will protect him.

"You probably should have invested in real security instead of these weak, silly trinkets." I say, swiping a hand out, knocking one of the idols off the shelf and to the floor.

His eyes widen as he watches it crash. "That was unwise," he says. "The spirits will be angry."

I just laugh at his attempt to scare me and turn the tables. But then a draft blows through, and one of the candles goes out.

Parlor tricks. Coincidence. Probably the AC kicking on—though I didn't hear a unit. I look around for an air vent anyway.

"Brian, maybe we should leave," Mina says, tugging on my arm. That absolutely will not happen. This loose end has to go, along with any paper evidence that might tie back to us. I know there's no paper trail around the payment, but there is that fucking master list Benjamin kept.

"Are you kidding me right now? You believe in this shit?" I say to Mina, not taking my eyes off our new target.

"I mean... no... but... I don't know... maybe..."

"I-I could read your cards," Benjamin says, clearly attempting to buy more time to live and to sway Mina against me.

"Mina..." I say, "he's a threat. He's already proven he can't be trusted. I don't do loose ends. You know this. And I'm not going to risk you for this fool."

"You should have all the information before you make a choice," Benjamin says. As though tarot cards count as information.

Mina takes her mask off and gives me the puppy eyes. Fuck. I swear.

"Fine, read my cards, but it won't change your fate."

I back off of him and remove my own mask as well as the heavy costume. I have a black T-shirt and jeans underneath and easier access to my weapons—exactly what I need with this slippery eel. I watch him carefully to make sure he isn't going to try some sleight of hand magic trick to gain control of the situation. If he sells so much of that shit, he probably knows how most of it works.

Mina also removes her outer costume. These costumes are fucking hot, and while they felt nice and cozy in the cold winter air, they are much more claustrophobic and stifling indoors.

Benjamin sits at the table and gathers up the tarot cards. They are black with intricately designed hyper real artwork. Pale alabaster nude figures are visible before he turns them face down and shuffles them into the deck.

"I need to add your energy to the cards, so cut the deck," he says.

I can't believe I'm engaging in this foolishness. But I cut the deck, trying to figure out what this guy has up his sleeve and how he'll try to wriggle off my hook. Surely Mina must know we can't leave this man breathing. That's the real danger, not his spooky ambiance and fucking tarot cards.

He holds my gaze for a moment, and then draws a card and lays it out on the table.

The Lovers.

I don't know what any of this means, but, The Lovers seems like a positive card, at least. The second card he turns over is The Devil.

Well, that's for sure me. No mysteries of the universe uncovered here.

The final card he pulls and flips over... The Tower.

His eyes widen a fraction as he takes it all in. I glance over to Mina and her gaze is riveted to him. Okay clearly The Tower isn't a good card, but who the fuck cares? They're just cards. They don't have any magic powers. They can't tell your fate or destiny. They're *just* cards.

Benjamin locks eyes with me and says in a way far more solemn and creepy than he should be able to with his life on the line, "Tell her before it's too late."

I feel Mina go still beside me. She's buying this shit. I know she is. I glance down to see she's unconsciously twisting her grandmother's ring on her finger—the one she was told has protective power.

Benjamin's proclamation is exactly the kind of vague bullshit you'd get in a fortune telling tent. No clairvoyance required to set ambiance, pull out some cards, and say something that sounds almost wise. He assumes I have some sort of secret and is just trying to sow discord so he can barter with Mina for his life. Not a giant leap to make with a sequence like: The Lovers. The Devil. And The Tower.

"Oh yeah? How about we read your cards and see what fate and all the powers that be have in store for you."

I take the cards from the table, insert The Lovers, The Devil, and The Tower face down on top, and shuffle them.

"Cut the deck," I say, sneering at him. "It needs your energy."

I see him swallow visibly now that he's in the hot seat. He cuts the deck and I pull and flip over the card on top.

Death.

I look up at him and smile. His eyes widen, the blood draining from his face as he sees his little stalling technique didn't work after all.

"The death card doesn't mean death! The death card doesn't mean death!" he says frantically, waving his hands in front of me as if performing some warding protective magic.

"Well, in this case it does." I pick up the sharp pointy knife that looks like a mini jeweled sword off the table and jab it into his carotid.

He grabs at his throat, his eyes wide. "That was a mistake."

Or I think that's what he said. The blood is gurgling and choking him, muffling his words so I really can't tell. He could have said anything. A moment later, he's dead, his sightless eyes staring up at the ceiling.

Mina snaps out of whatever trance she was sitting in just now. "Brian! My God, what did you do?"

"What I had to do. He's not safe to leave alive. He would have talked when the police inevitably came calling. He couldn't follow one fucking simple instruction. If he'd kept his mouth shut and just made the fucking costumes he wouldn't be in this situation. He has nobody to blame but himself."

Why am I justifying myself right now? I did what I had to do to keep us safe.

The cat yowls from the other room and gets a case of the zoomies, rushing in and out around our legs, jumping on and off the table, and on again, knocking candles over in her frantic surge of random craziness. There are far too many flammable things and fabrics in this room. It goes up into flames so quickly.

I grab Mina's hand, and we run for the exit as the smoke chases us into the main part of the shop. Then I stop, remembering that fucking list. I can't risk that it'll be spared.

I rush back behind the counter.

"Brian! We have to get out of here!" She's coughing and covering her mouth with one arm.

I pull out several drawers behind the counter, tossing things out behind me, until finally I find the list with everyone's information. I toss it on the flames and watch as the fire consumes our costumes and the list—the only evidence tying us to the scene of the crime.

The investigation on The Yuletide Slayer will inevitably hit a dead end and the city will be talking about something else as soon as the new year rings in.

"Come on!" Mina shouts at me. She manages to pull the fire alarm as we run from the burning shop.

We get in the car, and just as I'm pulling out, the black cat crosses right in front of our path.

"Brian," Mina says after we've been on the road for several long minutes.

I take a deep breath, still shaky and paranoid we might be forgetting something... and half worried we may have been seen at some point.

"Yeah?"

"What did he mean back there? What he said? Tell her before it's too late?"

I sigh. "Mina, for God's sake, he didn't mean anything. He doesn't know anything. He's not psychic. He knows I'm a killer, and he wanted to play on your sympathies to try to spare his own life. And clearly it worked."

Well, not the saving his own life part, but he did his damage tonight.

"I don't think you should have stabbed him with that thing. It looked like some sort of ritual knife. And then... the cat, and the flames and..."

"Mina... that guy... I think he was some sort of mentalist or illusionist. He clearly runs in those circles. He's picked up some tricks of the trade along the way like cold reading and getting inside people's heads. He probably had something set up so he could make that breeze and candle thing happen to freak out people who come to the back room for a reading. He was just using your fears against you."

She stares out the window and doesn't say anything else, but I know she's still thinking about it and what dark secrets I might be withholding from her. And once a seed like that is planted, there is nothing on this earth that can dig it out.

12

MINA

I'm sure I'm going to see Benjamin Barker's sightless eyes in my nightmares for a long time to come. I've never felt bad about someone we've killed before, but Benjamin wasn't a bad guy. And he wasn't an immediate threat to our life. He just had a poor slip in judgment and paid the highest price for it. Would he have talked to the police? Maybe. Brian is right about the risk, but I can't stop thinking about how it all went down, how scared he was, how he begged... and Brian's complete lack of mercy.

And then there's all the magic tools. I know Brian doesn't believe in that stuff. And I'm not sure if I do. I glance down at my grandmother's ring. I mean... I wear it all the time, so don't I believe in that stuff just a little bit?

Surely I don't wear it all the time just because I think it's pretty.

The Lovers. The Devil. The Tower.

The cards were lovely and unusual. I don't know a lot about Tarot, but I'm familiar with the traditional Rider-Waite deck that most people think of when they think of the tarot—at least I'm

familiar with what it looks like and the names of the Major
Arcana, the twenty-two themed cards most people think of first.

And while this deck was clearly based upon that one with the
same card names, it had a very different look.

They were so beautiful. They looked hand-painted. Such a
tragedy for art like that to go up in flames—which is why I
grabbed them. They're still gripped tightly in my hand, and I'm
not sure if I got them all.

I don't know why I took them. I definitely didn't want a
trophy from tonight, but I just couldn't let them burn. It all
happened so fast. I don't think Brian knows I have them. I unzip
my duffle bag and slip the cards inside, hoping I'm not missing
any and desperately wanting to look at them. But it's too dark
inside the car anyway.

The few cards I saw in the shop all had pale nude figures that
looked as though they were carved from marble on a stark glossy
black background. Simple. Elegant. Hyper-realistic. Both the
lovers and the devil had highly erotic imagery but with opposite
intentions: one of love and one of bondage. The tower was a
glass reflective building, suspended in space, exploding into
shards, a tiny nude figure falling off the top, plummeting to his
doom.

I make a mental note to look up these cards and their meanings when I get home. Though their meanings seem pretty self-
explanatory. I'm not sure that I'll mine any new depths with an
Internet search.

And then the death card—a skull with a black and silver
snake slithering through the eye holes. I wonder if Benjamin
would have died tonight if that card hadn't been on top—if I
might have been able to talk Brian out of it. I feel like there is
some awful fate coming for us, and I can't shake it.

Did this fate get set in motion by Brian's actions tonight... or
was it already in the cards? I think it's strange that all the cards

that came up both for Brian and for Benjamin were Major Arcana. None of the suits, and that's the majority of the deck. What does that mean? Maybe it means he doesn't shuffle his deck well enough. That's what Brian would say about it, anyway.

I watch the scenery out the window, trying to clear my head of all of this morbidness. Christmas Eve is supposed to be a time of excitement and wonder and anticipation, a time to wait for Santa to deliver your presents, a time to leave out milk and cookies and maybe sneak a few yourself.

But tonight has been more macabre, morbid, and scary in its own way than Halloween, and as we've just moved past the solstice and are rushing headlong into a new year, I can't help but wonder what the future holds for us.

I'm surprised when Brian doesn't drive us back to the house but instead to a very nice suburban neighborhood—a wealthier neighborhood with large but not too ostentatious houses. Each house has tasteful white Christmas lights on the outside and electric candles in all the windows. There was obviously a meeting to determine how everyone would decorate.

And while it's a little boring and anal retentive for every house to be exactly the same, it's also pretty impressive—both because they got every owner of every house to participate, but also because this level of sameness on this scale is very appealing to the eye.

It's such a huge shift from the costume shop and the Krampus run.

"Brian? Where are we going?"

"Just one more thing I've got to do," he says cryptically.

It can't be another job. He would have told me. Besides, it's well after two a.m. on Christmas Eve. Surely even killers take Christmas off.

He parks the car and reaches into the back seat to retrieve a brightly wrapped package I hadn't noticed.

"Brian?"

"It's nothing. Stay in the car."

I watch him break into the house. Nothing smashes or breaks. He's got a key. Why does he have a key to this house? *How* does he have a key to this house? I'm worried an alarm will go off, but nothing happens. This is the kind of neighborhood where every house has a home security system.

As if to put a fine point on this observation, I notice a small sign in the front yard with a spotlight on it announcing the company that protects the house. And yet... no alarm starts blaring.

Maybe it's a silent alarm and the police will come to cart Brian off for... leaving someone a Christmas present? Maybe it's a bomb. I'm honestly baffled.

Five minutes later he's back in the car.

"That house has a security system," I say.

"I know. I have the code," he says as he backs out onto the main road.

"Are you going to tell me what all that was about?"

"Nope."

I turn back to the house in time to see a small boy looking out the window into the night. He's looking up at the sky like he thinks he'll find Santa Claus up there, and that's when I realize who it is.

"Brian! You're keeping tabs on the kid?"

He shrugs like it's nothing. I know I'm not going to get more out of him tonight on this topic, and maybe not ever. I lean back in my seat, stealing quick glances at him when I think he's not paying attention. Parts of Brian are changing. It isn't just with me.

Despite his impulsive darkness and the death he dealt to others tonight—the death we both dealt—something is changing.

But it's an additive process. I don't think he'll ever wake up one morning and decide to do something normal and boring with the rest of his life. He's never going to attend a City Council meeting to discuss the value of preserving the old historic trees on Main Street or volunteer to read to toddlers at the library—unless it's necessary for recon. He'll always be a killer. But he's becoming something a little bit more. And yet... I worry that the fate that may hang over us will snatch this new Brian away from me before he can take full form.

He turns the heat up until it feels like springtime in the car. I didn't even have to say I was cold. It's these small considerate gestures that get me the most, that make me think he is so much more than what he appears to be.

Finally he sighs and says, "Do you remember back in September when you woke up to the murder wall, and I admitted I'd killed someone without you?"

"Yeah?" I say it so cautiously, so quietly as though he's a deer I don't want to spook. I know if I push him he won't talk about this. I can tell it makes him feel vulnerable to admit whatever this is—even to me.

"It was Aidan's aunt. She was hurting him."

I don't know what to say to this that won't just re-trigger his own childhood traumas, so I just say, "Is he safe now?"

"Yeah, I think so. He thinks he's got an angel watching over him."

"Well, you kind of are." I'm still so shocked at the level of interest Brian has taken in this kid, going so far as to leave him a gift from Santa. It's surreal.

"No, you," Brian says. "He thinks you're his guardian angel. He told me when I was playing Santa."

I did see the kid, which was why I slipped away to another part of the store for fear he might recognize me. I wasn't worried for Brian with the fake white beard covering up so much of his face.

It takes everything in me not to make the kind of noise you make at the discovery of a cute puppy. But I keep it together. We're silent the rest of the way home. I don't know which fact is causing the puppy reaction in me. That Aidan thought I was an angel? That he told Brian? That Brian patiently listened to him tell his secrets? A combination of all of it?

When we get home we shower together, but we don't go run on the treadmill. It's far too late at night for that and everyone will be up bright and early for Christmas. Phyllis goes all out with the food for the holidays. And I wonder if Benjamin Barker has family who are about to have Christmas ruined for them for the rest of their lives.

I lie in bed in the darkness, the tarot cards and Benjamin's warning playing over and over in technicolor in my head. I want to brush it off as Brian does, but I guess I do believe in fate. And I feel that surely, given who we are and what we do—what we've *done*—that mine and Brian's can't be good.

EPILOGUE
AIDAN

T*hirteen years later.*

"Your father killed your mother."

It's the whisper of an almost forgotten memory. I wonder if it was even real—if she ever really said those words. I have only the vaguest memory of my Aunt Eliza. I was young, almost six at the time. I remember she was mean—to both me and the dog—but then one day she was gone, and Baxter and I were going to live with Uncle Martin and nobody ever told me why.

Baxter died two years ago. He lived a long happy life, but he was already three when I got him, and fourteen is ancient for a golden retriever. I cried for two weeks over that dog, though I would never admit this to a living soul.

I'd wanted to live with my uncle to begin with, but the system doesn't care what a kid wants. They think they know best. But if I'd gotten what I'd wanted without the detour to my aunt's house, I never would have had that dog.

That whisper in my mind lives with me. It haunts me. It goes to sleep with me. It wakes with me, and I wonder if it's true. Even though I have so few memories now, I loved my dad. But what if he killed her? How could I love him if he killed her?

I wonder if I inherited something dark and twisted that will make me do the same some day. All the men in my family are criminals. And although I haven't been formally inducted into the family business yet, I've done my share of bad things already.

I got my trust fund early—six months ago—so I could live on my own. I'm supposed to take over the business when I turn twenty-five. That's still six years away. I feel like I'm in limbo, just waiting for my life to begin. And I wonder if this bit of early financial freedom isn't really isolation and a trap. Maybe Uncle Martin isn't ready to hand over the reigns of power just yet. Maybe he hopes I'll fuck up, land in prison, and then he can keep the whole thing running. I can't inherit anything from a jail cell.

I've already had some close calls with the law—problems that just mysteriously disappeared as though someone watches over me. I glance at the dresser to the framed pen and ink drawing, signed with a mysterious Q.

My guardian angel. I would have forgotten what she looked like—and probably that she'd even existed by now without the drawing. I got it for Christmas that same year from... Santa Claus. I mean, I know it wasn't actually a jolly magic old guy who flies through the sky. But I've turned it all over in my head a thousand times now and still can't make sense of it.

My uncle took me to see Santa at a local department store soon after I went to live with him, and I saw the angel who protected me the night my dad was killed. I thought of her as an angel. Somehow my little kid brain re-imagined her as some kind of magical being who was watching over me and protecting me from the monster with the gun that night.

The day I went to go live with my uncle, I remember getting on the bus after my aunt threw a vase at me. It hit the wall instead. I sat there praying as the bus pulled away to be able to get away from her. I asked the angel in my head.

And then, to my complete shock, I never had to see my aunt again. When I saw the angel at the store, I tried to talk to her, but she moved too fast. And then Santa was back, so I told him.

On Christmas Eve, I woke to sounds downstairs. I don't think I was really fully asleep because I was trying to stay awake to catch Santa in the act—to find out if he was really real. He knew my name, so that felt like proof, but I wanted more.

When I heard the noise downstairs, I got up to go check. But by the time I got to the living room, there was no one there. I did see a new gift under the tree that wasn't there before. It was the only one of all of them wrapped in a different color of paper that actually said "From Santa" on the label.

I raced back up to my room to look out the one window that might give me a view of reindeer flying across the sky, but the sky was empty except for the bright glowing moon. Then I looked down to see a pair of car headlights disappearing around a curve.

I went back and brought the gift up to my room. Whatever it was, I wanted it to be my secret. Inside the box was the building kit with magnetic dinosaurs that I asked Santa for, which felt like full and complete proof of his existence—at least to a six year old. And then, underneath that, was the drawing of the angel. I remember thinking maybe Q was the elf at the workshop who drew her.

I kept the drawing hidden for years. I'm not sure why, but I didn't want to explain where I'd gotten it or who it was. It was my guardian angel, and I somehow thought the magic wouldn't work if anyone else knew about her. Maybe she'd stop watching over me if I told someone about her or showed them her picture. So I kept everything hidden until I moved into this house.

I know now that she wasn't really an angel. And there's another darker truth about all this and how it came to be that I can't let myself acknowledge just yet. I wonder if it's silly to have this drawing sitting out in my bedroom like this. Have I finally outgrown her and the comfort her image provided all those years?

The rest of my family prayed the rosary over an image of the virgin Mary. I did all my praying to the angel, and sometimes, even though I know it's stupid, I still do. I don't know how all the bits of luck happened throughout the years, all the things that protected me from danger or kept me out of trouble, but I know it wasn't magic.

Before I can decide if it's silly to keep the drawing sitting out in the open like this, there's a knock on my front door.

"Yeah?" I say warily when I open it. I squint against the sunlight. It's my first time seeing it today.

The man standing on my front porch is tall and muscular, dressed in all black. He has killer's eyes. I know because I've seen eyes like this plenty of times. I have eyes like this. The words out of his mouth confirm my suspicion.

"Hello, Aidan, my name is Brian Sloan. I'm the man who killed your father."

I immediately go into fight or flight. Has he been stalking me? Why is this man here on my doorstep right now?

My immediate thought is that my uncle wants me gone. I pull my Sig from the back of my waistband and point it at him.

But then I freeze as I hear another gun's slide rack. And then a voice I shouldn't remember, but I do.

"I would be very careful about what I did in the next few

minutes. We're here to make you an offer, and I don't want to be a giant cliché, but it's one you can't refuse."

I'm about to try to turn to look at her, to see if it's really her. But then the motherfucker who killed my father speaks again.

"You should probably put your weapon down. My girl is well trained, and, well she does have a gun six inches from the back of your head. Haven't you ever heard of locks?"

I'm about to answer when she answers for me. "You'd be so proud. He's got locks, a security code... but nothing I couldn't break through. He's even got a couple of guards on the property. Or had. We should find out who to send flowers and condolences to."

I can't believe these two are just bantering right now like a couple of psychos. She killed my security team like it was nothing, without an ounce of remorse.

I slowly put my gun down, keeping an eye on the man who calls himself Brian. "Coming to kill me before I can kill you, you motherfucker? Don't think I haven't been looking."

And I have been, but there isn't much to go on. And this whole time I had a clue right under my nose, a drawing of one of the killers. I feel so fucking stupid right now.

"Let's go inside and sit down for a chat," he says, like we're a couple of old friends about to catch up over coffee and pie.

When we get inside, I turn around and finally get a look at her. She's barely aged since the time of the drawing. And it was definitely her. My angel isn't a guardian angel, she's an angel of death.

I fight to keep the tears of betrayal out of my eyes. I am not going to cry like a fucking child right now.

"It's not her fault," Brian says. I zone out and miss half of what he's saying because the rage is starting to cloud my vision, starting to make my heart race. I catch something about her wanting to save me that night... "So if you want to hate someone, I'm your guy," he finishes.

I glare at him, not sure I can just switch gears and hate the symbol of all my childhood hopes, the person I sent all my prayers to, convincing myself she was a higher being who could answer them, and believing it that much more every time it seemed she had.

"Tell me, Aidan... how would you like to learn to be a real killer?"

I pause for a moment, weighing the options and remembering how my Uncle Martin always says to keep your enemies close.

"And you think you're going to train me?"

Seriously, what's with the pseudo-father routine? He killed my father. He doesn't get to swoop in and take up the role this late in the game.

"I trained her," he says.

I turn my attention back to the angel of death who does a slow turn, showcasing an arsenal of weapons attached to her body in various holsters.

"Okay," I say.

Brian seems pleased at my easy acceptance. "Good answer, kid. You're going to be glorious."

And then, the bomb drops and explodes, and the silent truth that had been clawing to get out of my psyche finally becomes loud enough for me to hear. It's the way he said 'kid'. Somehow out of a million almost forgotten memories, I hear that store Santa saying kid in this man's voice, and the obvious truth reveals itself.

I guess once I'd gotten older and realized she wasn't magic, I'd thought maybe the store Santa had told her about me calling her an angel, and she'd somehow gotten the drawing to me. He did know my name after all. I reasoned maybe the guy playing Santa knew my family.

But it was my father's killer the entire time.

I don't know how long this fucker has kept tabs on me or why, but I'm going to find out.

BEHIND THE SCENES WITH KITTY

Hello my little Holiday Sugar Cookie,

Welcome to the "director's commentary", or "Kitty rambles about her story to people who feel compelled to read every word in a book, including author's notes."

You chose this fate, my friend.

I told you we'd get into Brian's head for the Halloween pumpkin patch scene! And I really loved getting inside his dark and twisted mind for that. It feels like a really strong opening scene. One of the things I wanted to establish more strongly is that Brian's evil isn't so cut and dried like a cartoon villain, even though when he first appears in Guilty Pleasures, I literally wrote him with the intention of him being a one-dimensional cartoon villain to make the other guys at the house look better by comparison.

But as the story deepens with Brian and we learn about his childhood trauma, and his unfolding relationship with Mina, it starts to become clear that a lot of what we define as evil in him is a kind of wildness, an animal nature that he turns himself over to, and one that he isn't always entirely fully in control of.

This obviously doesn't excuse some of his more evil actions, but there are times when he's calculated and times when the wild takes him. The Pumpkin Patch is an example of that animal thing taking him over where he can't find the space inside his brain to have a rational thought, which is why he's so afraid to let go with Mina. I felt it was important to have a scene like that so it's clear that his fears around her aren't "crazy or irrational." There is a very real chance he could go over the deep end and kill her, even though she means so much to him.

Yuletide Slay Ride was complicated to write because there was so much I had to account for, and all that stuff is happening right in the middle of some complicated relationship issues between these two. The problem was... how do we do all the things that need to happen in this novella or at least need to be referenced due to the story overlapping the events of Surrender from the original Pleasure House books, while also dealing with what's going on in their relationship?

And how in the fuck do we fit it into a novella? I know... you're like... "Who exactly is 'We?'"... well I mean, me and the writing gods... obviously.

Back in Broken Dolls on the "unseasonably warm day" that Brian kills Jason (one of Mina's "bad masters" from her past), that's the same "unseasonably warm" period where Gabe goes out with Julie initially.

Gabe rescues Julie from a human trafficking situation and brings her to the house in late September during the events of The Massacre Ball and then the overlap continues through Yule-tide Slay Ride. I had to decide what to include in the actual novella and what to just put in exposition because either way it's part of canon and needs to be either shown or referenced due to the level of crossover for these timelines.

I also really enjoyed getting into Brian's head for that side of the scene with Julie in his dungeon. That scene from her perspective is one of my favorites in Surrender. And I think what's actually going on in Brian's head for this part is definitely unexpected if you've already read Surrender. I think most of us (including me) just assumed he was being his normal evil self.

Happily, this is where the Pleasure House direct crossover ends. Twisted Fates, from the original Pleasure House series happens "years after Japan", and so therefore also years after all the events of the Holiday Hits. So My Violent Valentine will be free of having to contend with any crossover events and we can just focus on the one timeline/storyline. Yay!

There is a moment in Twisted Fates that is relevant to Holiday Hits though... this is a small spoiler so if you haven't yet read that one, you might want to skim past this or go read it first and then come back here to my commentary. When Brian has Shannon in his dungeon again and Lindsay tries to use a threat against Mina to get Brian to let Shannon go, Mina says she can't get between Brian and what he does. "There would be consequences." To which Lindsay replies: "You think he would hurt you?" She says, "I don't want to find out." Whereupon Lindsay calls her a coward.

You might recognize this as an allusion to the events in The Massacre Ball where Mina did in fact interrupt and get in between Brian and "what he does", which resulted in him chasing her with a chainsaw. So... she knows.

There is an Easter Egg in Yuletide Slay Ride from my book "The Con Artist" that some super fans probably picked up on. The Con Artist occurs in a separate story world from The Pleasure House books, but we already have crossover with that world in Twisted Fates. If you've read The Con Artist or Twisted Fates, you'll recognize Quill, the artist who draws Mina for Aidan.

In Twisted Fates, Mina is very much aware that it doesn't

matter how much Brian cares for her, there is a very primal thing in him. And that thing isn't always responsive to her. So while she loves him and knows he also cares for her, she knows on a certain level she's always dealing with a caged tiger, and something could always go wrong.

It's not personal and is no more malicious than a lion chasing down a gazelle, but still, you don't want to be that gazelle.

I feel like this author's note is all over the place with just a list of random shit I like, but I'm just rolling with it. If you're still here, I appreciate you!

I love the Santa stuff in this one, both the interaction with Brian and Aidan as well as the Christmas Eve gift leaving and then the epilogue flash forward where we see the Blowing Things Up epilogue but this time from Aidan's point of view. I also thought it would be hilarious for a kid to pee on Brian because I'm demented like that. I enjoy putting him in weird circumstances you wouldn't necessarily imagine he would be in and then watching him untangle himself from those situations.

I also loved writing the scenes at the Benjamin Barker Costume Company, and the scene with the tarot cards. The tarot cards in this book are actually loosely inspired by a deck I own called the Trueblack tarot which you can find at trueblack-tarot.com (I get no affiliate commission or anything like that. I just think it's a TRULY beautiful deck. I own both the black and the white decks and would buy any deck this artist created. They are works of art and I'm way more precious and careful with them than I am with my everyday decks which are more like worn and well-loved stuffed animals.)

Originally in the first draft the cards burned in the shop, but it wasn't just Mina who hated to see them burn. I couldn't stand it either, so I decided she takes them. I'm not sure if or how the cards will show up in the last novella, but they may make an appearance. And I definitely wanted to leave that option open to myself.

I love that Mina sticks a syringe in Brian's throat in this one. Pretty ballsy, given what he is. But she's hit her limit with his emo crybaby bullshit. Dark and terrifying Brian is a million times more attractive and enjoyable than mope-y self-recrimination Brian. Originally I had planned that they would have a bit of a reversal of roles but there wasn't room for it in the story (It would have slowed down the main plot), and it felt forced, at least in this particular novella. And by removing it, it made the cafeteria Krampus scene more intense.

I always want readers to feel like "FINALLY!" when anything sexual happens in one of my stories. I don't want people to skim or be like "Oh, sex again..."

And... Brian Sloan not being his real name... we'll come back to that in the final novella. Don't worry, I didn't let that thread drop.

I had a hard time figuring out how to write the Krampus run kill, but was really happy with how it turned out. And I love Brian's ruthless nature coming out when two Krampus demons grab Mina and he just takes them both out John Wick style.

I also loved being able to use the Stryker building again from Blowing Things Up. I think it's great anytime you can re-use a scene/location across a series because it makes the world feel more solid. If every place the characters ever go is some totally new place within a city, it can really start to feel unreal. I often don't name my fictional cities, instead calling it "the city" because I don't like using real cities (I don't want to have to research the layout or have readers say: "Hey, there is no X on Y street!") I also don't often make up fictional city names because I just think it's a boring meaningless detail. Though since I have so many stories now in this world, maybe I should have named the city.

The epilogue with Aidan is the last "future" peek into this world and sets up Aidan's future book or books so the next time you hear from Aidan in "present day", it's going to be in his book. (And I don't know when that is coming. It's up to the writing gods.)

So I think that's about all I have to say on this one. Stay tuned for the final installment of Brian and Mina's Holiday Hits... My Violent Valentine. I can't wait to share it with you! This is the story I've been building to and what inspired me to do this whole series. If at any point you've thought: "Yeah, but why do they even need this side series?" That question is answered very clearly in My Violent Valentine.

Be sure to subscribe to my newsletter at kittythomas.com to get a free ebook and keep up with all the things.

Thanks so much for reading and/or listening, and I'll talk to you in the next one.

Love,

Kitty ^.^

ACKNOWLEDGMENTS

Thank you to the following people:

Robin Johnson of Florida Girl Design for the cover art.

My alpha readers: Lindsay M. And Morgan B.

One Night Stand Studios for producing the audio (coming Summer 2024)

Lori Jackson for Teaser Graphics.

My VIP Dungeon Pleasure House tier: Jill, Emily, Tish, Konnie, Allison, and Ashley.